D0029206

Leapfrog

and Other Stories

GUILLERMO ROSALES

Introduction by Norberto Fuentes

Translated from the Spanish by Anna Kushner

A NEW DIRECTIONS BOOK

Published by arrangement with the Heirs of Guillermo Rosales.
"Leapfrog" was originally published as *El juego de la viola* (Ediciones Universal, Miami, 1994).

Manufactured in the United States of America
Published simultaneously in Canada by Penguin Books Canada, Ltd.
First published as a New Directions Paperbook (NDP1267) in 2013
ISBN 978-0-8112-1941-9
New Directions Books are printed on acid-free paper.
Design by Erik Rieselbach

Library of Congress Cataloging-in-Publication Data
Rosales, Guillermo.
[El juego de la viola. English]
Leapfrog and Other Stories / Guillermo Rosales ; translated from the Spanish by Anna Kushner.
pages cm
"A New Directions Paperbook Original."
I. Kushner, Anna. II. Title.
PQ7390.R665J813 2013
863'.64—dc23   2013022652

10 9 8 7 6 5 4 3 2 1

New Directions Books are published for James Laughlin
by New Directions Publishing Corporation
80 Eighth Avenue, New York 10011

Contents

INTRODUCTION

The author of the two books that make up *Leapfrog & Other Stories* did everything he could so that none of this would make it into the reader's hands. His favorite method was fire. I know of at least two great novels and an epic poem totaling over one hundred pages that he threw into the flames. I think it was, above all, an act of courage and not of madness. And I don't think there's anyone else in the world, beside his sister Leyma, who can speak with authority about Guillermo. After having written the last word of each of each creation, he seemed to give them a certain life span, and if in a given period of time his editor (or anyone else) didn't show any interest, then he condemned them, without hesitation, to the flames. It could also have been a reflection of the visceral disdain he felt for the world around him. Destruction at the end of the torturous path to creation seemed a relief to him. But no one knows about the books I am referring to because no one read them. I had had before me the novel *Socrates* and his epic poem *The Hero of Yaguajay*, about Commander

Camilo Cienfuegos (I can still hear his evil, mocking laughter when he said, "If they only knew I'm doing an imitation of Quasimodo!"). And I had read his novel about the origins of Cuban rum and the wars of independence, with that amusing episode about General Shafter's landing on Daiquiri Beach, to the east of Santiago de Cuba. And I'd read the story, "Colonel, it's Puny Speaking," and another novel no one talks about but that concerns a battle against Batista on an imaginary mountain in the Sierra Maestra—la Taguara—with Camilo Cienfuegos again as the main character. I can't believe none of them exist now. Worse still, these stunning and unique literary works did exist and not even their ashes remain. Can you imagine what American literature would be without a Poe or a Wolfe, or French literature without Baudelaire or Camus, or Russian literature without Artsybashev or Akhmatova, just to name the most secretive and hidden writers? Well, then we Cubans have to accept our own national literature without Guillermo Rosales.

Our friendship began on his first day of work as a journalist for the magazine *Mella*, in the summer of 1961. He was 15 years old and hadn't read Hemingway, much less Faulkner, but he gave me a run for my money with his encyclopedic knowledge of the great Will Eisner's *The Spirit*. It was our shared culture as Cuban kids who grew up in the 1950s. This is tangible on the pages of *Leapfrog*, a book written by Guillermo very early in the 1960s and which he ended up naming very differently from how we first knew it in its initial Spanish edition. It was originally called *Holy Saturday, Resurrection Sunday*. It escaped the bonfire because Delia, his loving mother, went around picking up the pieces of paper and wrinkled sheets that her son left lying around as he was writing. The stories in *The Magic Still* have a different history. Guillermo was already living in Miami when he sent them to a friend in Washington so she could organize them and make a clean copy. In the editing process, Rosa Berra, the friend he'd known since the 1960s in Havana, made a digital transcription (computers were beginning to take over the market) and that is how the book was saved. We can assume that in 1993, when Guillermo made the decision to destroy himself, he wasn't going to leave his unpublished books at the mercy of unknown hands rummaging about.* So he proceeded, with as much disdain as meticulousness, to burn the thick bundle of his novel about rum and Cuba's liberators and any papers he had left in his drawers. Later, he put the barrel of a gun to his temple, metal that was cold to the touch. A Cuban exile community which doesn't understand him and which distorts him (and in the end, can't stand him) has yielded few readers. Perhaps he did well to throw it all to the flames.

NORBERTO FUENTES

---

* He committed suicide on July 9, 1993

LEAPFROG

At one, leapfrog,
At two, my shoe,
At three, go for coffee,
At four, hit the floor,
At five, I'll dive,
At six, breadsticks,
At seven, the razor's edge,
At eight, I'll beat you straight,
At nine, you'll be fine,
At ten, start again,
At eleven, get in on the action,
At twelve, an old lady snivels,
At thirteen, a midget can be seen,
At fourteen, an old man is clean,
At fifteen, I'll get your spleen,
At sixteen, run from that ox so lean!

LEAPFROG

April 12, 1957

It was the big night: the infamous Luthor had made a pact with the Men of Clay. Pat Patton was calling Dick Tracy urgently on his wrist radio to confidentially communicate Breathless Mahoney's secret: Darling O'Shea, the richest and most spoiled child in the world, was having fun on Black Island removing The Blank's masks. The Spirit was dying, pecked at by that vulture Mr. Carrion, but he reappeared in the next story chasing after Splinter Weevil, "The Meanest Man in the World." Everything was like that. The island was made of cork and would never sink. The West Side Boys raped fat Tubby and crucified Little Lulu in Hunchback Alley.

Tapón was living in his mountain house at the time and Denny Dimwit insisted on trying to launch himself to the moon in a barrel. Mama Pepita was withering away amid her childhood photos and Papa Lorenzo was dreaming of the dynamite train full of Stalin's Cossacks and meanwhile ran his finger over the cartoon page of the *National Daily News* and said, "This country really likes its comic strips."

In any event, Felix the Cat had taken flight dangling from a question mark. Mr. Hubert strolled through the park with his dogs, and Aunt Dorita was complaining that boys in the tropics were spawns of criminality.

"I'm a .45 pistol," the story from *Paquín* magazine read. "I'm made of hate. Hate. HATE."

Gaspar Pumariega had just then put up a giant television tower that deeply disturbed Don Mestre, the Channel Six magnate, and he appeared on the screen at night wolfing down chorizos with bread and raffling off Philips blenders.

Grandma Hazel, like the witch in "Macabre Stories," was stirring her cauldron with a slotted spoon and terrified Agar with Jehovah's finger. She believed in God but in the meantime, voted for the Communist Party even though she knew that if they won, the communists would put an end to her door-to-door food delivery business.

Meanwhile, in the far-off West, Wild Bill Hickock was having his definitive duel with Wyatt Earp, and Dean Martin was recovering his lost honor on the banks of the Rio Bravo.

The neighbors were sleeping at Santa Fe beach. The television sets and radios weren't on, and the pressure cookers had cooled off on the kitchen tiles. Manuel Castillo, the night watchman, gave a lazy yawn on one of the park benches and then let his gaze fall over the dimmed houses. In one of them a boy was dreaming of monsters from outer space; and on the other side of the world, a mongoloid child was masturbating alone amid lotus flowers.

At One, Leapfrog

There was the fall; Tommy Tomorrow's spaceship had broken down in space and they were all falling into the void. It was always like that. Falling, falling, and then the abrupt awakening. Waking up terrified in a pool of sweat, with the sheets stuck to his body.

"Grandma Hazel, why do I always fall when I'm sleeping?"

"It's Jehovah letting go of your hand," Grandma Hazel would say.

"Papa Lorenzo, why do people fall when they're asleep?"

"That has to do with what they've eaten," Papa Lorenzo would say. "Chickpeas are bad for you."

But now Agar was falling just the same. He had eaten lentils that night and was falling just the same into the void, kicking at nothing, trying to grasp at invisible branches.

"Wood, Wood!" Tommy Tomorrow's voice carried across 6,000 miles.

"Wood here."

"Wood, I think we're crashing. We've fallen into a bottomless abyss and we're being dragged by a meteorite belt—"

It was always like that: falling, falling, and then the abrupt awakening. Sometimes he saw the beach's lights from afar and heard the roaring of the sea and fell from the Coney Island Ferris wheel.

He fell toward the white floor of the amusement park and he could see the operator's stupefied mouth opening like an immense red O and the frightened eyes of the children in the bumper cars. He would fall and never reach the floor. When there were just a few inches to go he'd awake abruptly, in the darkness of his room bathed in sweat. Outside, stray dogs barked. In the distance, he could hear the noise of waves breaking and then dragging over the sharp rocks: *splashhh!*

He saw a shadow move on the other side of the door. Then steps and the red light: *click!*

It was Papa Lorenzo. He was asleep, dragging his hands along the bathroom wall tiles for balance. He walked naked in his sleep, and now he was going to urinate asleep over the toilet. Agar half saw him and turned his head away. It shamed him to see his father urinate and then shudder with the last drop.

Papa Lorenzo urinated for a long while, leaning on the wall, and Agar thought he would never finish. Then he shuddered, turned off the lights, and staggered on in the darkness. At last, Agar heard him fall like a dead weight on the bed and kick furiously against the sheets. Then all was absolutely dark again.

Behind the window, out came the old witch from "The Black Cat" to look at Agar, smiling sadistically. Twin vampires waited in the yard for their wooden stakes. A large spider web came down, like a fisherman's net, from the ceiling. Around his bed jumped the bug-eyed imps from the Cantarranas River. A donkey with a man's head galloped through the park.

He felt someone touching the sole of his foot with long yellow fingers, and he covered himself completely with the sheet. He must have looked like a dead man in a London morgue.

The old night watchman turned his head to better hear Big Ben's bells: *clang, clang, clang!*

"It's twelve," Count Dracula said, touching Agar's back with a long nail. The count's claw. The count's fang.

Agar was shaking. The witches surrounded him from all the

corners of his room. Every crack in the wall became a monster skinned alive by a uranium bath: "If I open my eyes, I'll see them, I'll see them, I'll see them. My God, when will the night end!"

The night was crushing him. Full of visions—white like a ghost's sheet.

Then silence.

"Your cousin Genovevo was a terrible boy," Grandma Hazel said, suddenly appearing in his memory. "Spoiled like you, he even raised his hand to his mother. May God forgive him!"

Mama Pepita stared at him coldly from the sofa. Aunt Dorita and Hubert's wife also stared.

"The last time Genovevo raised his hand to his mother, do you know what happened?"

Agar was trembling. He didn't want to hear Genovevo's story. *"Genovevo was a shithead!"* he screamed inside his head.

"His whole arm froze," Grandma Hazel said seriously: "Frozen like a stick. And when he died, they had to saw it off to bury him in a box as God decrees."

That was the story of Genovevo. Although it was also the story of Basilio, the boy from Tia Dorita's town whose tongue reached his navel. All because one day he yelled at his sick mother. Mama Pepita nodded her head.

"Sick," she reiterated bitterly. "And tell him, too, that whoever says filthy things, his tongue will also turn purple for the rest of his life. Purple and long."

Agar touched his tongue in the darkness.

It was there.

It seemed harder and longer than usual. He tried to speak and a hoarse sound came out. He would have cried for help—

women and children first—but Papa Lorenzo would have gotten up, staggering, and said, "What in the hell is wrong with the
damned kid? Can't I even sleep in this house?"

Agar held back his scream and felt himself sweating under the
blanket. He knew that if he uncovered himself, Genovevo would
be there, with his sawed-off arm, right next to Count Dracula, the
Creature from the Black Lagoon, and the Spider Queen.

At Two, My Shoe

"Get up!"

Mama Pepita woke him up abruptly. He greeted the day without any covers, legs spread wide, and everything coming out of
his underwear.

He felt embarrassed.

Before, he didn't care and was even a bit of an exhibitionist,
but now, with that hair there, he had left innocence behind. He
knew it.

"You urinated again on the toilet seat last night, huh?" Mama
Pepita reproached him. "Then I sit down and get myself all wet,
huh? But the boy doesn't care about that, huh? He just cares"—
she shook him by the shoulder—"about him, him, him!"

It wasn't me. It wasn't me. "Oh! My God, what an idiot! Yes, it
was me."

She looked at him severely.

"Get up already," she said, and turned her hunched back to him.
Now the day begins. Get up and look for your shoes. You have a terrible

urge to spit. Dry tongue, but pasty around the mouth like horse's drool. As if you had spent all night running around.

"Get up. Put your pants on."

I don't want wide-legged pants. My clothes move around me like I'm wearing a barrel. I like them really tight, like Red Ryder or The Headless Horseman.

I like the Headless Horseman. But I like Bat Masterson more. Although I think I would also like to be Bat's son with a big dog to defend me. And pity anyone who tried to …

"Now Rin Tin …!"

"What are you saying?" Mama Pepita yelled from the kitchen. "Get up already, I told you. You have to take the food to your grandmother's house. And then, you're going to get me Sensat cooking oil. And then …"

They will be so jealous of me. My God, how jealous they will be! Papa Lorenzo popped his head out the bathroom door.

"I'm in here," he warned. "So no one come in."

It was very different when Agar was inside, sitting on the toilet or under the shower. If anyone came in he had to curl into a ball and feel as if he were being pricked by a thousand pins.

Papa Lorenzo is full of mystery. He has false teeth, but takes great care so no one knows. Now he's fat and bald, but before he was thin.

Before, Grandma Hazel says, *your father used to dream about Russia.*

He went to jail because of Russia. He got shot in the shin because of Russia. He was obsessed. I have a picture around here of the 1940 strike. Thin and well-groomed. Wrapped in a red flag, with his eyes looking up to the heavens and his finger raised: Saint Gregory, announcing the gospels. *Russia is there, in the Heavens!*

From behind the door, Agar could hear Papa Lorenzo gargling.

"He's a monster," Agar thought. "Like that, when he's just gotten up, he's horrible. But he's more horrible when he hits me. Then I'd like to kill him. Although one day he'll pay for it all."

"Hey, dude," the West Side Boys say at the park, "Who here hasn't thought about killing his father, even if just once?"

I'll kill him. I'll kill him! I swear to ... (to whom would he swear?) *I can't swear to God. I don't believe in Him.*

One day, I wanted to make the sign of the cross to see what was going on with me. *In the name of the Father, and of the Son, and of the Holy Ghost,* I went around saying it, when Papa Lorenzo came out from behind the oleanders with his belt off and coiled to strike.

"Amen!" he said, and at the same time he got me on the back with the belt.

"I don't want to see you doing that again," he warned me later. "Get that into your head."

He hates God. He often tells God to go to hell.

"When you see him, let me know!" he says. "I'd like to meet the son-of-a-bitch who invented all of this."

"Forgive him, Lord!" Grandma Hazel shouts from her steaming cauldron.

No. I cannot swear to God. Although I can't swear by my mother either. It's easy to swear by your mother and not really mean it.

"May my mother fall down dead, it wasn't me, Mrs. Caritina," I said the day I broke the hardware store windows. And then I ran back home and Mama Pepita was behind the pots and pans, alive and kicking, as always.

"Where were you, you little devil?"

Swearing is stupid. Nothing ever happens. Although Papa Lorenzo has a system for swearing. It has to do with Stalin.

"Come here; did you take money from the dresser?"

"No."

"Would you dare swear to it on Father Stalin?"

And then he goes to the Closet of Souvenirs and brings out Stalin's picture and puts it on the bed.

You cannot swear by me in vain, Stalin seems to be saying.

"Swear!" Papa Lorenzo commands.

At first I would confess. But now the West Side Boys laugh when I tell them the story.

"Dude, your father is so ridiculous!"

So it doesn't matter to me anymore. I swear by Stalin in vain, although at times I discover him staring at me hatefully from his frame.

"Last night I dreamed I was falling from a cliff," Agar said.

Papa Lorenzo looked at him from over his breakfast mug without speaking. Mama Pepita went to get the crackers. Agar would have wanted Papa to say: *Really? So how did it happen? Tell me. Tell me all about it. Detail by detail.*

But Papa Lorenzo said: "Everyone dreams. That doesn't mean anything. Hand me the sugar."

Holy moly. I have to get away from this house. One day I made an escape map. The bedroom, living room, kitchen and the bathroom hallway. Someone left a window open. So I got away. I got lost in a wealthy neighborhood, and in the end, was taken in by a rich family. They wanted to adopt me. They named me "Friday," because the day I went on the lam was a Friday. They loved me so much! They had a pool and everything. Like in that movie with …

(what's that guy with the big nose called?) David Niven! *My Man Godfrey*. And Niven ends up marrying June Allyson.

Damnit! Would anyone take me in? Although in the end, it was horrible: Papa Lorenzo found the map with the warning signs. He laughed for a long time, the map in his hands.

"An escape map! Ha, ha, ha!" His belly shook. He turned red with laughter. Then suddenly, he got very serious and said: "There's no need ..."

He went to the front door and opened it.

"Go!" he said. "You want to leave, right? Go!"

I was shaking at the table. Papa Lorenzo was pointing at the horizon with his finger and Mama Pepita was grumbling in the kitchen. In the end, Mama went over to the door and shut it.

"Leave him alone!" she said, tired. "Leave the damned kid alone ..."

"Don't get involved in this!" Papa Lorenzo roared: "You're the one who has ruined him."

They exchanged insults loudly for a long time. Finally, Mama Pepita turned her hunched back and left sobbing for the Trunk of Photos of her Youth. There, she started going through the old photos.

"This was me at fifteen," she murmured, "or was I sixteen?"

She held the photos, looking at them for a long time, until she seemed to forget her troubles. Then she got up: "What a house, my God!" she exclaimed. And with that she went back to the kitchen.

Agar watched Mama Pepita go through the Photos of her Youth and listened to Papa Lorenzo searching through his Closet of Souvenirs.

"You'd be wise to burn everything in that closet," Grandma Hazel advised. "One day they'll come, search the house, and then we'll have to take your clean clothes to the prison at Castillo del Principe."

But Papa Lorenzo didn't answer. He shot her a hateful glance from his Closet of Souvenirs and brusquely took out a book from the bottom of a trunk.

"And you, Madam … do you know who this is?" He showed her a book with an owl on the cover.

"I don't care," Grandma Hazel said, pushing it away with her hand.

"It's Prince Kropotkin!" Papa Lorenzo said in a tired, irritated voice. "What about this one?" "Less still," Grandma Hazel answered, slightly nervous.

"Bukharin! The Benjamin of the October Revolution!"

"They're very well known in their own way," Grandma Hazel pointed out, with dignity, "but Jehovah is much larger than all of them."

"Madam …," Papa Lorenzo then said in a serious tone of voice, "I don't want to see what happens to you when the train of the Revolution blazes across this island."

"I'll be sure not to stop until I get to Australia!" Grandma Hazel laughed.

"A great train full of dynamite, with Lenin and Stalin's star on it ready to crack down on the old home food delivery vendors…"

"Don't forget that my home food deliveries pay for your food …," Grandma Hazel reminded him, while slowly wagging her witch's finger.

"Bah!" Papa Lorenzo exclaimed, picking up Bukharin and company and putting them back in place in the Closet of Souvenirs. "Humanity is a bitch!"

Agar rushed his cup of café con leche. Papa Lorenzo flipped

through the newspaper, saving the comic strips for last. Seeing his belly flow abundantly over his belt, Agar remembered Flattop, Dick Tracy's fattest enemy, who had died devoured by a barracuda in a Chicago pool.

Later, he remembered Grandma Hazel, wrapped up in the steam of her cauldrons, always repeating the same refrain: *Strange. Your father is strange. First he picked up votes, organized strikes and went around to meetings that always ended in gunshots. He even convinced me to vote for the Popular candidate! But now it turns out he's a Rotarian! He's a communist and he belongs to Rotary International! It's a strategic matter, he says. Strategic? I don't understand anything!*

Papa Lorenzo stuck his nose in the National Daily News stories.

"This country really likes its comic strips," he said in a low voice.

From the kitchen, Mama Pepita let the pots fall thunderously.

At Three, My Coffee

"What's up, Doc?" Bugs Bunny said. He popped his head out of the hole and patted Elmer Fudd's shoulder, who replied: "We're going to the land of giant carrots!"

Mama Pepita arrived with the hot food containers.

"Go to your grandmother's house," she said. "Have her tell you what she has for lunch. And here, give her this money. But hang on to it! Don't come to me later with an *oh, I dropped it!*"

"You come straight back here," Papa Lorenzo said. He was chewing a piece of bread with his healthy molars.

Straight. You come straight back. You go straight there. You go straight. Everything is straight. Straight to the point. What do they care if I stay in the park with the West Side Boys! Playing leapfrog, throwing stones or making up stories. What do they care! Then they say because you're too thin, and they smoke there and talk dirty. But what dirty things could they say that I don't know? I know them all! And I smoke, too. All the brands. Anyone who doesn't smoke is a fag. Anyone who doesn't curse is one, too. That's the law. That's the law and they'll never understand!

He took the containers of hot food and left. He made the trip to his grandmother's house kicking a stone the whole way. Three blocks to the right lived Mr. Hubert. "The one who always takes his dog out to piss," Papa Lorenzo would say, seeing him pull the leash. "If I were like that, I'd shoot myself." At the end of the block, between the pine trees, lived "The Abominable Man from Eighth Street."

"That miserable specimen spends his whole life watering his garden."

"Leave the man alone!" Mama Pepita would scream. "You spend your whole life hating humanity."

Amid the pine trees, lived Aunt Dorita, always seated at the piano.

"I never had any parties," Aunt Dorita would say as if she were telling a funny story. "My first party I was 22. I spent all week saving money to buy myself some crêpe paper ruffles that you added to the dress and looked like silk. I saved six pesos. I bought them. Grandma watched everything from her rocking chair and pressed her lips together.

"Hmmm," Grandma said, "so you're going to a party, huh?"

"Yes, grandma."

"And who gave you permission? Come on, come on?"

And then I said to her: "But it was you yourself, grandma! Don't you remember?"

To which she responded: "I don't remember anything."

"Grandma, grandma, how could you not remember now! I already told the boy yes and he's coming to get me this evening."

"Well he'll leave exactly as he came," grandma said. "You wasted all of your money buying nonsense and now we won't be able to pay the electric bill this week!"

"He told me he would lend me the money," I said. And grandma leapt indignantly from her rocking chair and insulted me as she slapped me.

"Who does he think I am? Huh? The madam of a brothel? Let's see. Give me that dress! You'll see what I do with the parties at the Liceo."

"And that was my first party!" Aunt Dorita summed up, trying to laugh. "Isn't it funny?"

"Of course, dear!" said Mama Pepita, adding more sugar to her coffee.

"That's how grandma was," Aunt Dorita said. "Poor thing …"

And she bit her lower lip, and her eyes shone strangely, and Agar thought that he wanted to jump up and down, and scream: *Son of a bitch, son of a bitch, son of a bitch!*

"Poor Aunt Dorita!" Mama Pepita said when she left. "She was a prodigious girl, but she peaked."

"She's an unbearable loon," Papa Lorenzo said from behind his newspaper. "They say she has a thing with Poupett, the manager of Novo."

"Slander!" Mama said. And then, remembering, she added: "She had a divine right hand. At the age of five, she would get up at night to play Bach. Do you know who Bach is?"

"It's all the same to me," Papa Lorenzo said. "For me, Bach or front, it doesn't matter …"

One night, the West Side Boys covered Aunt Dorita's house with chickpeas and eggs. They made long peashooters with TV antennas and shot the chickpeas from far away. Aunt Dorita went to Agar's house the next day to tell the story.

"You suffer so much in this country!" she commented. "It's so different than Europe. Everything here is so embarrassing. Have you ever seen a more diabolic being than a child? The children of the tropics are juvenile deliquents," she said, and fanned her face, suffocating.

He walked. He remembered this story and later remembered the West Side Boys sitting in a circle on the grass in the park, talking bitterly about people.

"Your aunt is a lesbo, dude," Bones said that time. "She goes everywhere with Poupett. The other day, they went into the Society together and both had their pant zippers down. They were munching carpets!"

Laughter.

He remembered all of this as he walked. He spent his whole day remembering stories, words, faces, situations. When he passed in front of Hubert's house, an old lady yelled from the gate: "Lift your head up! Why are you walking with your head bent down?"

Why? Why did Agar always walk watching his own steps?

Why did he get tongue-tied in conversations with his friends? Why didn't he have a girlfriend and why did everything make him feel tremendously ashamed? Why, why, why?

One day you spoke, said the Voice of Memory. *One day, you went up to them and spoke for a long time. You were talking and laughing. You were laughing a lot and they made room for you. Oh, how you were laughing! I could swear myself to you right now, Marta. And I could dance with you for hours and hours, Elaine, Blue Moon.*

"Hey, dudes ... do you know the story about the parrot who saw a scar?"

You were laughing. Your laughter could be heard all over the beach.

And the wave behind you: "SPLASHHH!"

Then came the whistle. Papa Lorenzo's unmistakable whistle.

"They're whistling for you, dude ..."

"Like a dog, dude ..."

Papa Lorenzo welcomed you with his eyes narrowed. He had discovered the half empty bottle of cognac.

"So you drank it, didn't you? I buy it and it's the boy who drinks it, isn't that so?"

"Drunk," Mama Pepita said.

And you laughed. You took a beating, but you kept on laughing. And your tears ran down your cheeks, until your eyes clouded over.

Agar kicked the rock like you kick rugby balls. They said he had good hands to play rugby. But he had barely any weight.

"That boy is sick," Grandma Hazel said. "He's greenish yellow."

"He doesn't eat," Mama Pepita would say. "He doesn't like chickpeas, he doesn't like beans. He doesn't eat."

I don't eat, I thought. *Not chickpeas, not beans. The smell of that food disgusts me. I throw it out when I can. It disgusts me. It turns my stomach. God damn! But you guys force it on me.*

"GIVE HIM THE WHIP!" Papa Lorenzo yelled from the sofa. "THE WHIP, THE WHIP, THE WHIP. That's purifying." And later, while he still had his newspaper between his hands, he confessed: "I was raised fast, as fast as a train. And then I was a man and I worked in a pineapple field. I had to take my entire salary to my father: nine pesos. Nine pesos! Of which my father took eight and left me one. And that one ...!" Papa Lorenzo said raising his finger, "he gave it to me, saying: Save it, in case I need it!"

Grandma Hazel laughed at the story. Mama Pepita said: "What a beast!"

"That's how it was," Papa Lorenzo said. "Raised as fast as a train—and I haven't died. Nor am I missing an arm—or anything else."

At Four, Hit the Floor

Grandma Hazel was working surrounded by the steam of her pots. She always smelled like cod and spices, and as she stirred the bubbling pot, she hummed incomprehensible songs.

She turned around.

"Did you bring the containers?"

"Yessiree. And the money."

"Tell your father not to worry about the money. I know you're a little short with that whole business about your school. Although I still can't explain it all to myself. A whole life spent

21

on strike! Always against the rich! And then it turns out that he wants to put you in a rich kids school. *So he rubs elbows with them,* he says. Rubs elbows with the rich? I don't understand. I don't understand. I don't understand."

And she brought her finger thoughtfully to her chin. "God is more constant," she said. "And it would do you good to put yourself in God's hands. How long has it been since you went to church?"

Church, Agar thought. *Papa Lorenzo doesn't want me to go into churches. He boasts that he has never entered a church and hasn't died because of it. Although Grandma Hazel secretly takes me to the Jehovah's Witness Hall.* She grabbed the back of my neck and said to me: "This, young man, stays between you and me … okay?" And inside, the pastor gave me a warm welcome and even placed me by the pulpit. And later he opened his arms and started to yell: "FORGIVE HIM, LORD!"

"Grandma Hazel, why does he have to forgive me?"

"Don't pretend you're a saint." she says. "You know very well why. You have to shout loudly: FORGIVE ME LORD, until you feel Jehovah. Do you understand? Until Jehovah enters you and you feel that your vices have left. Is that clear?"

So he shouted: FORGIVE ME LORD! FORGIVE ME LORD! FORGIVE ME LORD!

But then a fit of laughter came over him.

"I couldn't avoid laughing," he said later, surrounded by the West Side Boys. "The laughter came with a vengeance."

"I don't play around with that," Kiko Ribs said. "With God and the saints, everything is different."

"An old woman appeared to Tony Pando one night and

showed him an ID card that said she was 'Our Lady of Mercy," Tin Marbán said.

"And I know a priest who rolls up his soutane when he plays soccer," Fat-Headed Jorge pointed out. "Although I also know Father Gasoline, who says mass while drunk."

"And they say that the crazy monk who lives in Choricera," Pipo Páez said, "bangs his own daughter."

"FORGIVE HIM, LORD!" Grandma Hazel said.

She made Agar kneel down in the first row, near the pastor's dais.

"I tell you that HERE is Jehovah TODAY," the pastor said with his arms spread open.

Agar was getting bored. He thought that around then the West Side Boys would be in the park playing leapfrog and crucifying spiders.

Agar pretended to pray, leaning his hands on the rail. The pastor passed next to him squeezing the heads of the faithful and shouting his slogans. The old ladies in the second row moaned and furiously blew their noses.

He furtively took out his knife and leaned on the wood. *Now or Never,* said his Interior Voice. His heart beat strongly, and he remembered then all of that about there being a Heaven, Hell, Purgatory, and Limbo.

Where would he go?

"I'll take Limbo," Kiko Ribs had once said. "It's neither good nor bad, and you spend your whole life sleeping."

Now! the Voice said.

So he scratched "COCK" on the wood and quickly put his knife away. No one had seen him.

The pastor turned toward the front row and grabbed him by the neck with his sweaty hand.

"FORGIVE HIM, LORD!" he shouted, and Agar felt saliva splash his eyes.

Later, when he'd let him go, they started to sing "Jehovah, I am your slave." And Agar imagined that Papa Lorenzo would have felt proud of him.

Grandma Hazel's head emerged again from the steaming pots.

"Today I've got *tamal en cazuela* and chickpeas," she said. "Come to get them at eleven."

"Well, I'm outta here."

"What's this about being 'outta here'? Keep an eye on the company you keep! The other day they came to tell me that you were going around saying you were broken. Do you know what someone who is broken is? A useless man. Who can't have women, or children, or anything. Your uncle Quirilio was broken. Poor wretch!"

Agar remembered Quirilio. He would arrive at the house wringing his hands and Mama Pepita would treat him like a sick man.

"I'm in love with a blonde," he would say. He always had a new love.

"That's great, Quirilio! You don't say, Quirilio? Congratulations, Quirilio!"

And he nodded with his head one, two, three times.

"Yes, yes, yes ... I'm in love with a blonde."

"He ended up hanging himself," she said, somberly. Grandma Hazel. With her skimmer, she reminded Agar of the witch in "Macabre Stories."

"Didn't you read the news in the papers? In big headlines: "Man frustrated by love puts an end to his life."

That really was broken! Truly broken.

"Well, I'm leaving."

"Take it easy. And come straight back."

Agar went back to thinking about the broken ones. Being broken was a big thing for him. In school they talked about broken ones, but it was different.

"Dudes; the guy who breaks has two balls as big as this," Tin Marbán was saying that day. And everyone wanted to break then. Because everyone wanted to have two big balls between his legs.

"In this country the most important thing is to have very big balls," Tin Marbán said.

And he had tried to break himself in the gym on Gago street, lifting weights with cement bags. But he soon got tired and couldn't go on.

I'm going to have to accept what I have, Agar thought. Although afterward, Tin Marbán came back tired from the gym, and changed his story, explaining that they grew until the age of twenty-one.

He patted his sac. No. They certainly hadn't grown very much. Although he weighed them with his hands every morning he never found much improvement.

That was when the news started to spread, and he could see it spreading and spreading until it came face to face with Grandma Hazel herself. Like when gonorrhea starts spreading.

"Everyone wants to catch gonorrhea in this country," Tin Marbán went back to saying. "Because, in this country having gonorrhea means that you're getting some."

He remembered Pacheco, Ictericia's son. That day, he arrived tripping over himself at the circle of boys and then smiled enigmatically.

"Gentlemen ... three shots in three days. My prick is on fire."

"What, dude?" several anxious voices said. "Penicillin?"

"Cirilo Villaverde, dudes. I've gotten gonococo, it's raging, raging, raging."

From the ground, Agar watched Pacheco speak and turned green with envy.

He wanted to get it! But, how?

Later, Tin Marbán again explained that everything came from the Pajarito neighborhood, full of sailors and Chinamen, where a woman named Julia Cacharro measured one's business beforehand to the inch.

He wanted to get it! He wanted a good case of gonorrhea with all his might. But ... he hadn't even seen one of those women!

So what if he went? So what if Julia Cacharro measured his business?

"Scram!" Julia Cacharro would say. "You're disqualified."

So that was when he decided it was better to roll the ball. Because rolling and rolling ...

"Rolling and rolling, I rolled near a hole. I stuck in my finger and it came out all red. What is it?"

"Your mama, dude."

Laughter.

"Yours on the floor."

More laughter.

"Your motherfucking mama."

More laughter. The laughter of boys under the sun. Agar crossed the park. The kids still hadn't arrived. The lizards were moving restlessly on the trees, taking out their red ties. The sun beat down hard on his shaved head.

The day was still beginning.

At Five, I'll Dive

"Let's travel in the Memory Spaceship," Woody Woodpecker said.

Wally Walrus and Attila the Hen were also going.

Agar started to to turn the page, but Mama Pepita showed up in the door to his room. Her eyes were sunken, as if she had been crying the whole time. She always looked like she'd been crying. But in reality she'd been in the kitchen. *Peeling onions*, she said.

"Mama ... do you always peel onions?"

"Shut up!" she said. And later added, "Go look for Sensat oil at the corner store." And she handed him the coins and the bottle.

"Afterward, I'm going to the park," Agar said.

The screams from the park were making him anxious. They cut his breath short. They made him sweat.

"Is the boy so impatient to get to the park?" Mama Pepita sang.

He thought hard about it. If he said yes, Mama would say: Then you have to stay at home.

It was better not to respond.

"Well," Mama said, "what are you waiting for? Get going!"

Then he had to cross the park with the bottle of oil.

It was hard for him to cross the circle of West Side Boys.

He started to walk, pressing his butt together, holding in his breath.

"The delivery boy, look at him … there he goes!"

"Dude, bring me a packet of crackers … would you?"

"Dude, in my house they're looking for a head maid. The pay is good and includes lots of food."

Laughter.

"Dude, is it true that in your house they tie you to the table leg?"

Something got stuck in his throat. Agar felt his penis shriveling.

"Hey, dude … we're going to swim in the Cantarranas River! Are you coming?"

Laughter.

Agar turned around. He was angry, but he tried to appear calm.

"Okay," he said. "Okay. I'll come right back. And then my hands will be empty."

"Oh what a good-looking dude! With his little bottle and everything."

Laughter.

"I bet I can break the bottle!"

"I bet you can't!"

"I bet I can!"

"Bet you can, go, go!"

"I bet you're not man enough!"

A chorus of angry voices. A drop of sweat slid down Agar's forehead and hung from his nose. Silence.

"Dude, what you said …"

"Men kill each other over lesser things, dude."

"Holy shiiiiiiit!"

Danger. He knew he had said something serious. Irreparable. He remembered Papa Lorenzo's order that day he came back with his face smashed up and his eye busted by a punch.

An eye for an eye.

Bones walked over to him. Agar's legs were shaking and he thought of breaking into a run. But he immediately understood that then he would never look the West Side Boys in the face. If he contradicted himself, he would also have to withstand their mocking laughter forever. Mocking laughter that he would hear at night, wrapped in a sheet in a pool of sweat.

If a fight started, he was going to lose. He knew he was going to lose.

"What did you say, dude?" Bones wanted to know, walking toward him. He spoke calmly, like one who is used to danger.

"I didn't ... I didn't say," Agar stuttered.

"So now it turns out he didn't say!" Bones exclaimed. "Come here, dude. Have you ever gotten a good correction?"

And he grabbed the collar of Agar's shirt.

Just then, Mama Pepita's voice could be heard from the door.

"What are you doing?" she yelled. "I told you to go straight there!"

"Leave him alone, Bones!" the chorus said. "Leave the boy alone ..."

"I'll get you when you come back, boy," Bones warned. "Get ready."

"Let go of me."

Mama Pepita's voice had saved him. He straightened out his collar.

"You think you're so hot, don't you? Because I'm going on an errand, right?"

He continued on his way. The sun was beating down hard on his head. From the park bench, the West Side Boys yelled at him again: "Cinderella!"

"Sons of bitches!" He muttered, swallowing the snot and salty water running down his cheeks.

Hubert's wife yelled at him from the gate again: "Lift up your head! Do you want to be a hunchback when you're older?"

Go to hell! He yelled in his head. He kicked a stone hard.

Then he remembered John Wayne's movie "The Quiet Man." Everyone mocked him because he was a quiet man. They mocked him. They mocked him. They mocked him. Until one day, John Wayne punched someone, just one punch, and he killed a guy. He had a forbidding right-hand.

Agar got to the corner store and leaned his elbows on the counter.

"A bottle of oil," he said.

"Look who's here!" The shopkeeper exclaimed. "The pyromaniac. Is it true that you burned down the Páez house?"

"Sensat," he said. "Sensat oil."

The shopkeeper went to get his order. Agar looked at him hatefully.

I hate everyone, he thought. I'm against the Indians, but also against the Cowboys. I don't have a mother or a father. An Indian named Pocahontas found me in the woods and raised me.

"That's seventeen cents," the shopkeeper said.

He paid. He took the bottle of Sensat oil.

For all your meals, Sensat.

But there was also Oliveite oil.

And he remembered the slogan: *Oliveite tastes so great.*

Tongolele announced it. A television star. With glorious tits.

"My God, those tits! Those tits!"

And they shook.

"They're not real," Mama Pepita maintained during the shows.

Papa Lorenzo looked at her out of the corner of his eye and said: "Ha!"

There were three cents left. He thought he should buy cigarettes.

"I know you smoke," Grandma Hazel would say. "I know you smoke with those little devils in the park. And there's more I know. I know sometimes you steal them from the Mini Max."

"Whoever doesn't smoke is a fag," Agar said.

"You wretch! You're going to bring your father down even lower than he is. You're going to send away your paralytic mother with a coronary thrombosis. You're going to bury us all. And you're going to end up a gangster. Gangster. Gangster."

I like the idea. I'd like to be someone like Splinter Weevil. The meanest man in the world. Everyone beat him as a child. He grew up amid blows. And rolling and rolling, he became a man. And one day he was picking apples in his father's orchard.

"Pick them up!"

"I can't. I don't feel well. Ohhh ..."

"Pick them up!"

"I can't. I don't feel well. Ohhh ..."

"Pick them up!"

And that was the end. Splinter sunk his hoe into his father's chest and then kicked his mother in the head, and stole the money that was under a bush. Then he got his ticket to Chicago.

Then came what happened with the bank. There was nothing easier for him than a good hold-up! First you disconnect the wires and then you calmly ask them to put everything in the sacks.

"The pigs!" Bones suddenly shouted. "We're dead!"

Splinter looked at him in disgust. He slowly put out his cigarette with his foot.

"Are you nervous, Bones? You're a chicken. I don't want pansies in my group, Bones—"

"No, Splinter, no!"

"I'm sorry, Bones ..."

KAPOW! KAPOW! KAPOW! KAPOW!

The sun was beating hard. Bones was dead. The pigs evaporated into thin air.

With the change he bought three Royal cigarettes. He would save them for later, when he was in the park enjoying the scent of the rosemary, looking at the clouds and imagining new ways of revenge.

On the way back he decided on a shortcut through Hunchback Alley to avoid the circle of West Side Boys.

At Six, Breadsticks

"Hey, dude!"

The voice of evil called to him as he passed through Hunchback Alley.

"Over here!" The voice said.

He thought it must be one of those closed circles that the West Side Boys made to read pornographic books.

"What's up, dudes?"

He saw familiar faces, but they were a little worked up.

"Dude, we have to show you something," Henry said.

Agar saw some of them smoking and lit up one of his cigarettes. He inhaled the smoke until he felt his lungs fill up. Seeing them smoke, some of them even smoking three cigarettes at a time, reminded him of Mama Pepita's indignant lamentations.

"It's not worth your time," Papa Lorenzo would say. "They are the 'Very Embodiment of Bad Ideas.' They all do it to go against the grain. But ahhhh," he warned, narrowing his eyes, "If I catch you playing that game, forget it. I'll kill you right then."

"Let's go over there," Agar said, letting the smoke go out through his nose. "I hope it's not something moronic."

"Come on, dude," Henry said, putting aside all bad intentions. "Don't you smell that, dude?"

"What is it?" Agar asked, intrigued. Though he couldn't deal with the stench anymore.

They went around the edge of the abandoned house. It had been a beautiful house, but now the West Side Boys had completely destroyed all of its windows.

They arrived at the place at last. The stench was unbearable.

"It's a dead mare," Henry said. "And she was about to give birth. Don't you see the bump, Agar?"

A swarm of flies was circling around the thing in question.

"She was about to give birth." Henry insisted. "She was tied up in Liborio's field and got loose."

"The captain killed her," Kiko Palacios pointed out, placing his boot on the swollen belly. "Godinez, the sea captain. Denny saw him driving his Buick when the mare got in the way."

"And he ran over her?"

"No. He got out of the car and shot her twice."

"I saw it all with my own eyes," Denny said, coming out from behind the wild rosemary. "Two shots."

"Son of a bitch," Agar said.

"I don't know anything about that, dude." Denny said. "Politics don't interest me. What I can tell you is that it was loaded."

Denny broke off a stick of rosemary and shoved it forcefully into the dead beast's sex. Agar shuddered in horror when the stick entered, breaking the flesh.

Henry leaned on his shoulders. Suddenly, Agar felt a great desire to hold that stick.

"Give me that stick, dude," he said, biting his lip. "I'm going to tear her apart."

He took the rosemary and sunk it in forcefully, digging into the orifice, until a trickle of whitish liquid came out.

"She came, dude," Henry whispered. "That's it! That's it!" And Agar felt the boy's hand trembling on his shoulder. The sun was beating down on the rosemary bush and a halo spiraled around their heads.

Agar felt two urges. One was tugging at his body, pushing him to run away from there forever. The other directed his arm, making him sink the stick in up to the hilt.

He felt disgusted, but strangely satisfied.

"Don't be stupid," he said later, throwing the stick far away. "She's dead."

Denny Dimwit sat down on the animal's swollen belly. He exhaled the smoke from his cigarette and said: "But that's how women work, more or less."

"But you have to get them there," Kiko Palacios assured them. "You have to 'know' how to get them there."

"Is it very deep?" Agar wanted to know. In his mind, he was calculating according to his own resources.

"Eight inches to the end," Denny said. "Although that varies. Eight, nine … that's where a woman's weak spot is."

Agar felt frustrated. It was too much. In the afternoons, he went into the bathroom at home where he'd hidden a geometry ruler in order to measure himself. And he wasn't any more than five inches.

"What are you doing with a ruler behind the toilet?" a surprised Mama Pepita wanted to know.

"I brought it in by accident," he replied.

He thought that if Mama Pepita had suspected anything, he would have had to hang himself from a lamp. Then his memories disappeared as Denny continued to explain: "Women, there are two kinds. Wide and narrow. Hot and cold. My mother, for example, is cold." A thousand needles pricked Agar's face.

"Why?" Agar asked.

"My old man says so every once in a while," Denny said, indifferently. "You're already a man, he says. I can talk to you man-to-man. Right? And then, he says to me: Do you know how long it has been since your mother and I did it? A month! Do you think that's fair? And then he says: Find yourself a Spanish woman for home; an Englishwoman to go out; and an Indian woman for a good time. What do you think?"

"Listen, dude," Henry said. "Your old man is really something!"

"He's a real joker," Denny said. He searched his nose with one finger and added, "A month ago, when I turned eleven, he talked to me in the living room like a friend. Son, he goes and tells me: you're already a man. And as a man, I'm going to tell you something. (And during all of this, mom is signing to him to shut his mouth.) He started to laugh and said: What you have there is not just for urinating, do you understand? It's to be used. Use it well! And at the same time, my old lady goes: Animal! But he kept on going as if nothing happened. He shrugged his shoulders and said: It's my duty! My father did the same with me. And his father and his. And so on and so on. And thus ... to infinity."

Denny Dimwit took a stick of pine and rolled it around in his closed fist.

"In any event," he said, returning to the matter at hand. "I'm in no rush. The thing grows until you're twenty-one. About an inch a year."

He let out the smoke arrogantly and added: "Mine will be legendary!"

And Agar felt himself being reborn. He turned around, touching himself between the legs. From eleven until he turned twenty-one, there were still ten long years. And Denny was calculating one inch per year. He patted his penis and felt it small beneath his clothes. He felt ashamed of how many times he'd imagined that it would never grow.

Like that day they were urinating on the park benches, and he was so nervous he had to take a good look because he couldn't get it out, and Bones had asked: "What, dude? Did you lose it?"

He finally ended up taking it out at last. Although he remembered that then the stream hadn't come and how nonetheless, that night, he had pissed all over himself in bed.

At Seven, the Razor's Edge

They were lying on the grass. Smoking under the sun facing the mare. The evil rosemary bloomed, and the West Side Boys broke into their space.

"A treasure!" Tin Marbán yelled. "The dudes found a treasure."

So they all explored the dead beast.

They spent a while jumping over her, until they fell on the grass. Pacheco's dog had come with them and was barking furiously at the putrefied corpse. Bones called her over and spit in her mouth and she swallowed Bones' saliva.

"Hey, speaking of, Dude, you know who died?"

"No."

"Well, someone who was alive."

Laughter.

Agar felt he was being mocked.

"Hand me a smoke, dude," Kiko Ribs said. And then he lit the cigarette, cupping his hand around it wisely. As he smoked, Agar recalled Mama Pepita the day she smelled his mouth.

"This boy smokes," she discovered, shocked. "He smells like an opium den."

He remembered previous episodes in a row. Like the day they found cigarettes in his shirt and Mama Pepita saved the box to show it to Papa Lorenzo when he got back from work.

That time he spent the whole afternoon shaking like a leaf in his room. And he had wished that someone would arrive that night with the news that Papa Lorenzo had been in a car accident.

By nine, Papa Lorenzo still hadn't returned, and then he thought he had killed him with his supplications. Deep down, he understood that he did not want to kill his father.

"You can leave him an invalid, okay," he pleaded, "but let him live!"

Deep down, he didn't really understand himself. He saw Papa

Lorenzo look up at the peeling ceiling and write names in the air with his finger, and he thought he loved him.

"I was raised by the whip," Papa Lorenzo said that time, looking at the walls stupefied. "My father went to get me on the ball field and ran after me around all the bases with a belt raised high.

"You have to work!" he would say.

Papa Lorenzo smiled faintly and continued: "I would have been a good Major League player. If it hadn't been for how malnourished I was, God knows where I would be now! Tom Casey saw me playing once and liked me. 'What a shame!' Tom Casey said. 'If he had another twenty pounds on him, I would hire him for Cincinnati.'"

And Papa Lorenzo nodded along to his words vehemently and said later: "Ha! ... I was a good center fielder."

So it was. Agar loved him sometimes.

Nonetheless, the night of the cigarettes, Papa Lorenzo arrived at last at eleven. Safe and sound.

"This is the brand you smoke, you addict?" Papa Lorenzo wanted to know.

"No," Agar said. He now regretted his moment of weakness. He understood that Imaginary Fate was now punishing his indecision.

"Dead or alive," Fate insinuated, "but not in between."

"Open your mouth!" Papa Lorenzo ordered, waving the pack of cigarettes in front of his face. "Open it! Open! Open it!"

"You're acting like a savage!" Mama Pepita shrilled from the sofa.

"It's this neighborhood ...," she muttered, "it's this country, this life."

Papa Lorenzo squeezed Agar's jaw and opened his mouth at last.

The cigarettes went in all the way to his throat.

"Swallow them!" Papa Lorenzo yelled. "Swallow them, you addict! You are the very face of Heresy ..."

Agar was choking.

Mama Pepita took him to the toilet between hiccups. He vomited a yellowish juice and ground tobacco. As he leaned against the wall, he remembered the "salt episode." Another time when Mama Pepita had ripped into him with her litany about his vices.

"This boy eats too much salt," Mama Pepita said.

"Let him explode," Papa Lorenzo recommended, looking over the comic pages.

"Don't you know that salt waters down your blood?" Mama Pepita scolded Agar him. "You're going to turn yellow."

Papa Lorenzo paged through the newspaper absentmindedly. He seemed very tired.

"I bet you don't care, right?" Mama Pepita suddenly spat at him. "The boy spends his whole day eating salt and you don't care if he explodes."

"What do you want me to do?" Papa Lorenzo yelled, sitting up. "Kill him?"

And at the same time, he jumped out of his seat and tried to look Agar in the eye.

"So the boy eats salt!" he said, as if repeating lines he'd learned by heart.

"He's addicted," Mama Pepita assured him calmly.

"Addicted? I know a way to get rid of his addiction."

Papa Lorenzo went to the pantry and came back with his fist full of salt.

"Have salt!" he yelled. "So you die of pleasure."

And he threw the fistful of salt into Agar's mouth.

"Animal!" Mama Pepita yelled. She ran over to Agar and thumped his back helpfully.

And Agar still didn't understand. It had happened just like the event with the toilet. Mama Pepita had also taken on two roles then: the Witch, and Pinocchio's fairy godmother.

"Pinocchio doesn't flush the toilet," Agar said.

Papa Lorenzo Stromboli jumped up again, tired of yelling.

"Why don't you flush the toilet, knucklehead?"

"I don't know ...," Agar tried to explain. "Sometimes I forget ... I don't know!"

"In your rush to go join your friends, huh? And now you're going to leave without flushing again, huh?"

And he pulled Agar by the ears.

"Get your ass over here!" Papa Lorenzo said. And Agar remembered the West Side Boys' voices, playing with his name: *"Get your ass here, Agar. Get your ass a cigar!"*

Papa Lorenzo led him forcefully to the toilet. Agar kicked furiously in front of the bowl. Papa Lorenzo said: "From today on, you will never forget."

And then he ordered Agar to stick his hand into the yellow bottom.

"Go!" Papa Lorenzo ordered.

When will you learn to flush the toilet? When will you learn not to smoke? When will you learn to not say filthy words? When will you learn to respect your mother? To wash your hands, brush your teeth, not to tell lies?

Agar hated Papa Lorenzo. He would have driven a wooden stake into him. Deep inside. The rest would be easy. Run away, run away, and come back at the age of thirty, when the crime had been forgotten.

"Hey, dudes … anyone here ever dreamed of getting lost and then coming back years later, suddenly someone important?" Tin Marbán had once asked.

"You know, I have a plan for that," he said later. "Change my hairstyle. Whoever changes his hairstyle changes his life. People even forget your name. You're somebody without a past."

Mama Pepita grumbled from the sofa without any specific reason. Papa Lorenzo was watching a clown show on the TV.

Agar was alone in the bathroom and when he looked at himself in the mirror, he admitted he was an ugly boy.

He hated himself. He hated his body and his face. And he hated himself inside.

You should die, he thought. And he took a razor. *It's just as easy as moving this blade across these veins.*

He swiped the razor gently against his skin, then pressed down until he cut himself a little below his wrist. He stopped there. Watching his blood drip slowly down his arm. But he immediately imagined that the blood was volcano lava and that the hairs on his arm were a legion of frightened Hair-Men.

"WE'RE SINKING!" the Hair-Men yelled.

The blood reached his elbow. The Hair-Men sunk. The clowns laughed on the TV.

"Change the channel, hon," Mama Pepita's indifferent voice said. "Put on Gaspar Pumariega. Maybe they'll give away some Philips blenders."

"That miserable fat man disgusts me," Papa Lorenzo said.

"He's the classic exploiter of monkey brains, like you."

Agar cleaned the cut with toilet paper. He turned his eyes back to the mirror and made a terrible grimace. Finally, he went to a corner of his room and laid down.

He closed his eyes.

From the living room, the clowns laughed. But he didn't hear them. He was now piloting a plane loaded with atomic bombs that he would later drop over the city of Havana.

At Eight, I'll Beat You Straight

The mare changed colors. She turned purplish under the sun's rays.

They were still lying in a circle around her, used to the unbearable stench.

"The one they're the strictest with is Agar," Tin Marbán said.

"They always beat me," you said. You laid back and added: "It's good for me. That way I get used to life's hard knocks."

But you were lying. You were trying to find some advantage to your disgrace.

"I wouldn't want to learn like that," Kiko Ribs said. "No, no. If my father beat me like that, I'd kill him."

"My father beats me when he's had a fucked-up day," Speedy said.

And the West Side Boys laughed.

"And he almost always has a fucked-up day," Speedy added, and the laughter continued.

"Here, all of us are fucked up," Tin Marbán opined. "It's the law. My father was fucked up by his grandfather. And my grandfather was fucked up by my great-grandfather. And my great by my great-great. And now my father fucks me up. And I'll fuck up whoever comes next."

"Hey, dudes … has anyone here ever thought of killing his father?"

Silence.

You kept looking at the rosemary. One day, in the garden, you had thought it. You thought that Mama Pepita was an oleander and your father a vicar. Mechanically, you started pulling up the flowers. Decapitating, dismembering, pulling the leaves off. Mama Pepita showed up at the door and yelled in horror.

"Murderer!"

The garden was ruined. It was a cemetery of petals and uprooted heads. At night, Papa Lorenzo pulled you aside.

"Come here, kid. You're quite a case. Would you like to tell me what you got out of breaking apart those flowers? What pushes you to destroy everything? What? What? What?"

Suddenly, he started to beat you. You moved back toward the wall, trying to cover yourself, without responding.

"Why did you pull up the flowers?"

"I don't know!" you yelled at last. "Don't ask me!"

"Fucking kid," Papa Lorenzo grumbled, tired of beating him. "Prison fodder."

And he stayed like that for a while, looking at Agar bitterly, but then later it seemed as if he were remembering something similar, from many years before. And he looked at Agar again, surprised.

And he smelled himself under his arms. And he slowly went back to his newspaper, scratching the back of his head.

43

At Nine, You'll Be Fine

The sun was beating down hard.

The mare's skin was stretched under the rays. Tin Marbán commented on it, looking at her: "She can't complain. She has a well-attended wake."

Figure out this riddle: it's not a cow, but it gives milk. It's not a submarine but it's down below. It's not a communist, but it leans to the left. And it's brave because it lives among pricks.

Who is it?

Laughter.

Everyone knew who it was. The joke was old.

"Well, dudes," Liborio said. "I'm going to make an announcement: I've been letting out the sweet stuff since last Saturday. I, Liborio!"

In chorus: Prove it! Prove it! It's so easy to talk the talk.

Liborio hushed the voices with his hands.

"Take a look at Mandrake the Magician," he said. "Nothing there and suddenly ... plop!"

And he took out his penis.

Agar looked at it, and was relieved to confirm that it was more or less like his.

"Hit it hard, dude!" The chorus said. "Henry will entertain you by reading something."

"*Chased to her Bed,*" Bones said, offering up a small, wrinkled book. "One shot!" he assured. "The dude's name is Quasimodo. And his instrument comes down to his knees."

Laughter.

Liborio rolled his eyes and lay down on the grass.

When there was silence, Henry started reading.

"In the town of Quivicán, where sin flourished, Quasimodo Pomarrosa was a women's masseuse. How many buttocks had passed through his hands! How many sighs of pleasure! How many lives ...!"

Liborio stopped rubbing himself and Henry stopped reading.

"What's wrong, dude?" the chorus said.

"Dudes ...," Liborio confessed, annoyed. "I don't want you to see my thing. That's what's wrong."

The West Side Boys let out a sigh of disappointment.

"It's better if you leave me alone." Liborio proposed. "I'll let you know right away."

So they left Liborio masturbating alone amid the pines and went back to the House of Broken Windows. To sit in a circle on the grass. In the middle of the rosemary. Under the sun's rays.

"Bones is giving it to Tubby." Kiko Palacios commented.

"How's that?" Speedy wanted to know.

"Easy!" Bones said. And then he explained, "You wait until the mother is sleeping. Around two. Then you go and, as if you didn't care, you say, Tubby, would you change two hooks for me? That's the password. He made it up himself."

"Two hooks ...," Speedy murmured.

"Two. And then, you end up getting it on with him easy."

Agar knew Tubby. He was the son of a family of silent Spaniards who walked around in espadrilles. He had a nine-year-old sister who spent her days sucking lollipops: Little Lulu.

He remembered the day that Tin Marbán came by telling one of his stories. He said he had found Tubby playing with dolls at the Cobas' house. But he said he had long suspected as much, because he could smell it.

"I have a nose for fairies," he explained.

So they all went to Tubby's house that afternoon. And his mother came out to welcome them and said, surprised: "Oh ... but today isn't his birthday!"

She seemed happy about the sudden friendship between the West Side Boys and her son.

"I didn't know Tubby had so many friends," she commented, smiling.

"We've always loved him!" Bones said, hiding a lightning conductor in his hands behind his back.

Fine. Tubby had gone out. Mrs. Cobas lent out her garage and the West Side Boys pretended to play at being a music band.

"Noise," Bones directed them. "Lots of noise, dudes ..."

Fine. After they drew sticks the ones who were lucky went in. Agar was happy enough to watch Tubby's white buttocks and to be making a ruckus to throw off Mrs. Cobas.

Fine. Fat Tubby knocked on Little Lulu's door. The West Side Boys knocked louder on some cardboard boxes.

"What do you want me for?" Lulu wanted to know, once in the circle.

"You know why," Tubby said. "Let's go."

"It's done ...," Bones said afterwards. "When she started to cry it was already over."

Laughter.

From the pines, they heard Liborio's voice.

"Hey dudes ... you can come." He was smug.

The West Side Boys went one by one to confirm the news.

"But, you can barely see it," Agar complained.

"Well, old man, I'm not a factory …"

Laughter.

"So what did you feel, dude?" Agar asked. He knew he was giving himself away, making his curiosity known. Tin Marbán had once come around saying he felt a great tickle, and Agar wanted to trick them, saying he had felt that. But the West Side Boys' chorus was implacable again: "Prove it! Prove it!"

And he couldn't prove what couldn't be proven.

"A huge tickling feeling, man," Liborio said, buttoning his fly. "And then you're just a ragdoll. All loose, like this …"

And he fell down on the grass dramatically.

"The first time, I passed out for an hour," Tin Marbán said, with a certain air of superiority. "It really hit me hard. Although in any event, I was already a man," he added, putting a hand on Liborio's shoulder.

The West Side Boys smiled, satisfied. They patted Liborio's wet back and yelled and cheered into the air, howling wildly. Agar envied them deeply.

The sun beat down on his skull and he wiped the sweat away from his brow with his hand.

Amid the ruckus, Kiko Ribs had the idea of hunting spiders and making them fight each other. They immediately looked for lizards. Alex hunted one down and then tied it to a spinning top. Then he looked for a hole in the earth and put the animal in it with a pine stick. Agar seconded it with a stake, that he would have to bury at the exactly right moment to cut off the spider's retreat. It was like fishing in the earth.

The spider bit, and Alex expertly started to bring it in. At the designated moment, Agar fit in the stake and the spider flowered amid the dry earth.

"Grab it!" Bones said. "Dare to grab it, come on …"

Agar looked at it, undecided.

"Like this!" Bones said. He put his finger on its hairy abdomen and grabbed its back legs. "Okay?" And made as if he were going to throw it at the group.

The day was very clear. The grass was extraordinarily green and the spiders were intensely black on the grass. The West Side Boys were making a coliseum out of paving stones. At last, they threw the spiders inside.

The two beasts tried to escape from the stone circle, but it was useless. Bones put them back in the middle just when they'd almost made it out.

"Fight, bitches," Bones said.

"I think it's a male and a female," Kiko Ribs pointed out.

"They should fuck then!" Bones decreed.

They all laughed.

The small spider began attacking and soon the two were in a furious embrace. The West Side Boys screamed loudly trying to cheer on the scrawniest one. Agar wanted the little one to win. After all, he felt like a sort of small spider in the middle of another grand coliseum surrounded by water on all sides.

"Bite!" Agar yelled in solidarity.

Just then Hubert's wife showed up, making her way through the rosemary. Apparently, she happened to be going by Hunchback Alley and the screams got her attention. She made a gesture of disgust and, noticing the mare, covered her nose.

"Animals!" She screamed. "Is this how you spend your time?"

Silence. The West Side Boys stood up and tried to act respectful. Later, amid the silence, Bones let out a noisy burp.

A chorus of laughter.

Hubert's wife tried to say something, but the laughter drowned her out. She turned red. Above the laughter, she managed to make an insult heard, and then she left, breathless.

The larger spider had won. With difficulty, it pulled itself away from the dead one and embarked upon a shaky withdrawal toward the stones. Bones let it climb up and then, he slowly crushed it with his foot.

They all fell down on the grass again.

They were happy. They were sweating like wild horses under the tropical sun and they were perfectly happy. Like the times they crucified lizards on the trunks of trees, hammering their legs in with pins.

"A high-level operation ...," Bones would say, slicing open their abdomens with a razor. And then, one by one, he would take out the animal's organs and put them on the grass.

"Hey, dudes," he suggested. "Let's transplant a lizard brain into a spider ..."

They were also happy injecting formaldehyde into frogs and watching them get thinner, eaten away by the poison.

"But the one who's breaking the record is the lizard I have at home," Tin Marbán said. "I've had it for eleven days in a matchbox without any food and it still sticks out its tongue when I pinch it. I want to see how long it lasts. There are camels that go five years without drinking any water."

Alex went over to the weeds and bent down to fix himself.

"All eyes on him," Bones alerted.

So they stayed still, watching Alex, waiting in silence.

"Your thing isn't coming out today," Claudio observed.

"Wait a little bit," Alex said. He moaned forcefully and finally the thing came out. A long organ that hung between his smooth, dark buttocks.

Agar turned his face and felt his insides turning.

"My mom says I have to get operated on," Alex said. "But with everything she has going on, she always forgets."

And he shook his organ from one side to another.

"My horse tail," he said. "My little lizard tail."

Laughter. Laughter. Laughter.

Agar silently begged for it to be over. It had been a long time since he had left on the olive oil errand and they might be looking for him already. He was afraid that Mrs. Hubert might have gone house to house telling a new tale about the West Side Boys, and that she would get to Papa Lorenzo with the story.

Like the time they urinated on the park benches and Hubert's wife had foolishly sat on one.

"Do you know what those little animals are doing?" she said, going from house to house. "Urinating on the benches! Where decent people sit down." And she snorted, furious.

"Don't worry, Mrs. Hubert," Papa Lorenzo said then. "If I see mine playing that little game, I'll take a gun and wham! Right down."

"Animal!" Mama Pepita reproached him later, from behind the pots and pans in the kitchen. "How can you talk that way about your own son?"

"Okay, okay ... I didn't mean to say it like that. Not that way."

Alex had finished. He put his organ back and cleaned himself up expertly with a *malanga* leaf.

Kiko Ribs went up to the mare and said: "Hey, dudes ... the skin is cracking."

Bones appeared amid the rosemary with a bunch of dried leaves in his hands. He went up to the animal and placed them around it.

"A crown and everything," he said. "Dudes … who has a match?"

Excited by the idea, the West Side Boys covered the beast with all the leaves they could find.

"Odin's pyre," Speedy said.

"Odin …," Bones pretended to pray. "God of all that's broken and of all we have to break in to 'get in.' Fire to the can!" he yelled, lighting a match.

"Until the bottom comes out!" The West Side Boys yelled in chorus.

They laughed and howled around the pyre. They listened to the cracking of the mare's skin and they jumped amid the smoke. Later, their spirits lowered for a moment. Kiko Ribs fell down in exhaustion on the grass.

"On Friday, I'm going to confession," he said, putting his hand up as a visor. "I'm going to have to tell the priest all about this."

Agar said: "I get the giggles when I'm in church."

"The same thing happens to me, dudes," Bones said, flopping down. "The day Little Mute Guy died. Do you all remember Little Mute Guy?"

The flames grew. Agar watched them, entranced, and remembered Little Mute Guy, sitting in silence on a park bench, wringing his hands until someone called him into the circle.

"Take good care of him for me," Mrs. Caritina said. "He wants to be one of you."

Later, in the circle, Bones explained the rules to him.

"To be like us," he said, "you have to be fearless, mute kid."

And they all laughed.

"You have to burn down houses, climb trees, piss far and wide and read the Count of Eros and see what you can get away with. Let's start: do you know how to climb trees?"

"Climb!" The Chorus said. "Make him climb!"

The boy went over to one of the trees in the park and began to climb, holding on to the thick knots. Agar saw him going up and heard behind him: "Go up, mutey, go up, mutey!" And he envied the affection they all felt for Caritina's little mute guy.

"He's not mute at all," Bones said. "He climbs like a chameleon and smokes like a bat. I don't see anything mute about him."

The little mute guy reached the top of the tree. From there, he seemed to make an attempt at a pirouette and suddenly they all saw him fall to the ground like a stone.

Agar now remembered the story and thought he saw Caritina's face bathed in tears. She was there, in the park, surrounded by the crowd, while Dr. Miranda took the boy's pulse and shook his head.

"He burst a vein in his neck," Dr. Miranda said. "He made too much effort to climb this damned tree."

"Always up in the trees!" Mrs. Hubert then said. "Like animals …"

Caritina didn't speak. She stood up and looked over at the group of West Side Boys.

That night, they saw her again during the wake. That was where Bones began to laugh, swearing that the Mute Guy had winked at him from his coffin.

"May you be damned a thousand times!" Caritina exploded when she heard them laughing and charged the West Side Boys furiously, issuing curses. Then they really did run away, frightened.

"Do you know what those little animals did at Caritina's wake?" Aunt Dorita came in saying that night.

"What now?" Mama Pepita listlessly asked. So Aunt Dorita told the story and looked at Agar with her eyes on fire, as if to say: *And you know you were a part of it.*

Aunt Dorita, Aunt Dorita ... why do you hate me?

"The children of the tropics are a bunch of delinquents," Aunt Dorita insisted. "Cruel and disgusting. You pass through a decent place all relaxed, and there they are laughing under their breaths. You go to a wake and there they are laughing at the deceased. You want to play the piano and there they are saying filthy things. Asses and tits. That's the only thing they think about! And you can't have any friends because straightaway they come up with some perverse story about you. And you pretend to ignore it! And you pretend you can't hear it! And you pretend you can't see it!"

Agar knew the origins of Aunt Dorita's hate. It came from the night on which Tin Marbán had come up with the story that she and Poupett had left the rosemary field together.

"That's enough," Bones had said. "Can we allow that on a decent beach?"

Amid the laughter, they all wagged condemning fingers.

"Today, we avenge our stained honor," Bones said.

So they bought eggs and peas at the corner store.

Núñez the Spaniard filled the bags and asked, amazed,

"Who is the party for? Why do you want so much?"

Without getting any response.

Later, they made the trek to Aunt Dorita's house, assigning

positions beforehand. When they were already on her block, Agar heard the keys of her piano and Poupett's broken voice singing "*Quiéreme Mucho.*"

"The two of them together…," Bones said, rubbing his hands together. "One aims and the other shoots."

And the shooting began. Eggs and peas. They all heard Poupett's voice go up a key while the shots increased in intensity. "*Quiéreme Mucho,*" as the eggs went crashing on the walls.

They were bombarding the house for a long while, and in the end had to stop for lack of further projectiles.

Then only Poupett's voice remained. Poupett's hoarse voice singing "*Quiéreme Mucho,*" and Aunt Dorita's piano in somber accompaniment.

Agar had fired hidden in the bushes. He would have died of shame if Aunt Dorita had discovered him amid the West Side Boys, with his pockets full of eggs and the peashooter under his arm. But Aunt Dorita didn't come out. Not even later, when the projectiles ran out and the insults began. At the top of their lungs, the West Side Boys vituperated against Poupett and Aunt Dorita. They expected them to come out and respond, but they only heard the piano and could see through the blinds their shadows lengthened by the flame of an oil lamp. The screams died out. Amid the music, the West Side Boys fell discouraged to the sidewalk.

"Let's get going," Bones ordered. They began their silent retreat through the rosemary. And that's how they left: beaten down, dissatisfied, disconcerted. Listening to Aunt Dorita's piano slowly grow quieter as they got deeper into the rosemary, along with Poupett's already tired voice, singing "*Quiéreme Mucho*" as if it were now a requiem.

That's how it went. He remembered it now as the mare went up in flames and they sat in the circle, with the sun beating down on their shaved heads. The fire was languishing.

Agar took the bottle of olive oil and got up. He sensed from one minute to the next, that the West Side Boys would begin to play rough. Jokingly at first, hard and serious later.

"At one, Leapfrog!" Kiko Palacios yelled suddenly, jumping over his head.

"I'm first!" Bones yelled before anyone else. He looked for a stone that was small enough to fit in his fist without being noticeable and crossed his arms to confuse things: Where do I have it?

The stone went around, alternating from hand to hand. The one who had it in the end had to be the mule and allow himself to be jumped over.

"Leapfrog" had once been played very nicely.

Mr. Hubert said that in his time, they had played it at school, and that even seminarians lifted their soutaines to jump. Then it was no more than simply leaping over a hunched-over kid's back, singing out the number of each leap. But with time, the West Side Boys had turned it into a macabre and painful game.

"Do you know how they play Leapfrog in the Santa Ana neighborhood?" Tin Marbán said that day. And then he explained the game just as they had all played it since.

The stone went through all of the hands until it reached Agar. When he looked back, he confirmed there was no one else left. So, he would be the mule and would withstand the leaps, hiding his head well between his shoulders, because Bones had already warned very loudly: "The head's for the Devil! And if my foot runs into your head, it's not my fault."

"At one, leapfrog!" Bones yelled, jumping over him and delivering a tremendous kick to his behind.

"At two, my shoe!" Kiko Ribs yelled, saying, "Gong!" and letting a big stone fall on his back.

"At three, my coffee!" Tin Marbán yelled, spitting a mouthful of water on Agar's neck that ran down his shirt to his underwear.

"At four, hit the floor!" Kiko Palacios said, digging his nails into his bony shoulder blades.

"At five, I'll dive!" Lefty yelled, pinching his back hard.

"At six, breadsticks!" Speedy said. And since breadsticks don't cause any pain, he threw a handful of mud on Agar's clean shirt.

"At seven, the razor's edge!" Liborio yelled, smacking his sides with the back of his hands.

Agar sinks his head. He lowers his back. He clenches his buttocks. He remembers Grandma Hazel the day she went by the circle of West Side Boys, stayed watching them play for a moment, and then said: "Children . . . why do you hate each other?"

"We're just playing!" they all exclaimed.

"No, no. You want to destroy each other. Do any of you know what a lung is? A lung is a very delicate things. As is the brain. A small nothing that can break at the slightest blow."

You spit on the grass. Your lungs hurt terribly and you thought you would spit a reddish drool. But no. White saliva. Thick paste like a horse's drool.

"At eight, I'll beat you straight!" Claudio yelled, whacking a spiny branch on his back.

You closed your eyes. You thought that by then, Papa Lorenzo would be looking for you because of the delay. Mama Pepita might have received a visit from Mingo, the corner store vendor, and would have put some money on number eight, saying, "Yesterday, I had a revealing dream: three dead men."

"Oh yeah?" Papa Lorenzo would say, pretending to pay attention.

"Yes," Mama Pepita would say. "Three dead men hanging from a *guásima* tree."

"So play 888," Papa Lorenzo would say, reviewing the comic pages.

The kids flew over his back again. They leapt at nine and at ten.

"At eleven, get in on the action!"

"At twelve, an old lady snivels!" And this time, Kiko Ribs coughed on his head and Agar felt the kid's saliva in his ear.

"At thirteen, a midget can be seen!"

"At fourteen, an old man is clean!"

"At fifteen, I'll get your spleen!"

Agar was worked-up. He was waiting for the last leap to start off a long run after the West Side Boys and grab one of them forcefully and beat any part of his body. Until it became nighttime.

"At sixteen, run from that ox so lean!" Bones yelled, leaping over him without putting his hands on his back.

They ran.

When he got close to Lefty, Agar punched his ears hard. Both rolled around the grass, embracing furiously. Lefty's hand took hold of his throat and Agar felt blood beating at his temples and his eyes popping out of their sockets. He had the kid's ear gripped tightly and tried unsuccessfully to get his teeth near it and to sink them into the ear lobe.

"Stop that!" It was Mr. Hubert. He had come with his dogs,

certainly because of his wife. He approached with his bulldogs and brusquely separated them.

Lefty and Agar looked at each other with hate for a moment. Huffing, dragging the backs of their wrists across their saliva-filled mouths, muttering indecencies. A minute later, Lefty crouched down and patted one of the dogs' backs. Agar went over to the bushes and urinated, then went back to the group.

Everything was over.

It was always like that: they beat each other with a blind fury and then forgot about it. Blows in the heat of the moment. Letting it all out in the heat of the moment. Against any face, anybody, anything.

Mr. Hubert looked at them in surprise. He looked around and discovered the mare covered in ash and dry leaves.

"Sons . . . ," he tried to say. "There are games that are a lot more fun. Less dangerous. The *quimbumbia*, for example, is a very animated game."

He took two sticks and banged them forcefully.

"Come?" he said then.

While he beat the "*quimbumbia*" stick, Agar remembered Papa Lorenzo saying about Hubert: "Hubert!" Papa Lorenzo would say. "He's just like Hubert, the fat guy from the comics! The same idiot face. Always taking his dogs out for a piss."

"Leave the man alone!" Mama Pepita would yell.

Hubert then said, "I brought you something." And taking a ball out of his pocket dramatically, he dropped it in the middle of the circle of kids and said, smiling: "Try to play peacefully, huh?" And, after winking first at them mischievously, he turned around.

The West Side Boys watched him go in silence. When he was far away, someone threw the ball up in the air. Agar understood that now dodgeball would begin. Throwing the ball hard as anything against anyone.

He tried to get away from the group, but it was already too late.

They were throwing it against him. Bones didn't throw it against Alex and Alex didn't throw it against Kiko Ribs either, and Kiko Ribs didn't throw it against Claudio, either.

They were throwing it at him. He was the chosen target.

"An eye for an eye," Papa Lorenzo had said that day Agar came home full of bite marks and pine-needle scratches.

"He's skittish …," Mama Pepita said, sadly, "like a horse."

Later, Agar knew all too well, time would pass and the wounds would turn into hardened scabs, and he would pull them off, curious to see his own blood run.

"Well," Bones announced. "You've got three strikes. We're going to execute you now."

For the execution, they chose a chopped-off palm near the House of the Broken Windows. Now he had to put his arms around it and expose his back to the ball.

"And go!"

The ball missed. He heard Kiko Ribs regret his bad aim and give Bones a turn.

"Strike!" Bones said. And the ball hit his kidneys and he felt his skin burning under his shirt.

"Don't start crying, dude …," Bones warned him. "That was just practice. That's all."

"Take a good shot," Kiko Ribs said. "The Núñez girls are coming down the alley. Make it good, Bones!"

This time, the ball hit the back of his neck. The girls went by the alley and saw him hugging the palm tree. With his face hidden he heard them laughing.

"Why don't you talk to those girls?" Papa Lorenzo would say, pointing far away. "Look at their asses, kid. Look how they're moving it. They like to show it off. At your age, I was devouring them all."

So Papa Lorenzo would tell about his Don Juan life in the village of Candelaria, where he had had a catalog of girlfriends.

"*One day you spoke to them,*" The Voice of Memory said. "*Don't you remember anymore?*"

"Yes ... one day I went over to them."

"*Of course!*" The Voice said. "*You did well. You took out a bottle of cognac and discovered the very taste of life.*"

Not just anyone can take a drink of cognac! Not just anyone can bear feeling their insides moving around! Not just anyone can keep from vomiting! But you withstood it. And your head was spinning. And you were able to talk to one of them ...

"One, yes. Yes, that's right. One is the one that matters to me. Just one and no other ..."

But Papa Lorenzo was waiting for you that night with his arms crossed.

"Drunk again?" He said undramatically. And he beat you silently, drily, like never before.

"That's not how you do it!" Mama Pepita protested from the kitchen.

"And how do you do it? Tell me! Do you know?"

He left and came back later with the Court of Patriots.

"Take a good look at them!" He said. "I want you to solemnly swear that this is the last time in your life that ..."

The patriots stared at him indignantly.

"Swear!"

The ball beat down on his back again.

Fine.

He wasn't crying. The girls had passed and were now far away. He felt the drops of sweat running down his thighs like lizards. Then he heard Papa Lorenzo's whistling. Papa Lorenzo's unmistakable whistling coming from Hunchback Alley.

"I'm dead meat," Agar thought.

He tried to run.

"You can't leave now, dude." Bones said, blocking his way. "You're paying your dues."

The West Side Boys had already made a circle around him. There was a circle for everything. For the spiders. To tell jokes. To take out their members and rub them madly waiting for a finale that never came. To smoke, to play, to piss, to fight.

"Stay still, dude," Bones said. Agar felt a swift kick and fell to the ground.

Papa Lorenzo whistled again from the Alley while Agar cried on the ground, with a powerful knee on his chest and a tough hand around his neck.

"Look at him crying!" Kiko Ribs said in a fag's voice.

"Leave him alone, dude ... here comes his father!"

Agar stood up, wiping his tears quickly away. Papa Lorenzo crossed the field of rosemary and went up to him.

"Who hit you?" he wanted to know.

"It was a game."

"Who was it?"

Agar looked at Bones without answering. The kid bent over, pretending he had a pain in his ribs.

"Hit him!" Papa Lorenzo ordered drily.

"We were playing …"

"Hit him!" Papa Lorenzo insisted. "I want you to fight him, you son of a bitch! Hit him!"

So they started hitting each other. Lightly at first. Hard and silently afterwards. Agar felt the rain of blows fall on his face and clenched his jaw without saying a word. He swept blindly at Bones' face, and sometimes felt that his blows managed to do damage. He cried silently. Without moving an inch of his face. When it was over, after insulting the West Side Boys, Papa Lorenzo grabbed him by the scruff of his neck.

"Go to bed, you son of a bitch!" Papa Lorenzo said once they were inside their house.

In his room, Agar heard Mama Pepita shuffling around the pots and pans in the kitchen, and from there came the unmistakable smell of chickpeas.

At Ten, Start Again

"'We're in the West, son,' Old Jerome said. 'And what you see here is none other than Tombstone: "The Two Who Refused to Die."'"

"You'll stay in your room," Mama Pepita said. Then she closed the door and left him alone in there.

Old Jerome started running to town. Agar turned over on the bed and thought that just about now, the West Side Boys would be running through Gómez Pass, hunting spiders or exploring the bushes.

His eyes scanned the room and he started to play with the gaps in the walls. Because, with the gaps in the wall and a little imagination, time flew.

The gap in the corner turned into Sergeant York, with his helmet and backpack. The peeling paint on the bathroom wall made up a legion of soldiers clearing the decks.

He would have liked to go to war. He would have liked to prove himself against bullets. He felt that only by turning into a hero could he free himself of his past. So sometimes he was Sergeant York, and other times he was Splinter Weevil, The Meanest Man in the World, and other times, he reappeared in Veracruz killing Indians with a revolver that never ran out of bullets. But that afternoon he was in Tombstone, Arizona.

He closed his eyes.

He tied his horse at the town's gate and spit on the dry earth. He would walk.

He had waited for this moment for thirty years. He adjusted his guns and started walking slowly. Reverend Cunnings was the first to see him. He looked up at the heavens and rushed to shut the church doors. The church bells rang quickly and everyone in town ran to their windows.

"It's Lorenz's son!" They yelled from the Saloon. He heard the poker tables moving around loudly and the pianola waltz languish. He remained there, with his legs spread wide, standing in the center of the main street. Time seemed to stop in Tombstone. Tumbleweeds rolled by on the empty street.

They were scared. They were all scared. Only Parker the judge, leaning on his crutches, dared to look him in the eye.

"Listen, Bronco ... listen to the words of an old man and then do whatever you want. But ... may the devil take me away if it wouldn't be right for you to forgive!"

"Where is he?" he said.

"Pop Lorenz left here a thousand years ago. May the devil take me away if that's not how it was. He might have gone to Yuma," Old Parker said, looking nervously at his pistols.

"Get back!" Bronco Joe said brusquely.

"Listen to the words of an old man, son!" The judge exclaimed, feeling found out. "Forget about the past ... I know you can do it!"

"Forget ...," Bronco Joe whispered. "It's hard to forget!"

"Leave it be, Parker!" He heard behind him. It was the unmistakable voice of Pop Lorenz.

He turned around brusquely and saw him again for the first time in thirty years. Tears of indignation threatened to fall.

"Leave it be!" Old Lorenz repeated. "God knows I don't regret a thing!"

He grabbed a fistful of dirt and threw it at Bronco Joe.

"That's what you are!" he yelled. "Dirt!"

Bronco smiled wanly and said: "The same old Lorenz, right?" He rubbed his chin, thoughtfully. "I'm glad it's like this," he said then. "It resolves an old doubt I had." And he let the words fall lightly: "Do I kill you ... or not kill you?"

"So what did you decide?" Pop Lorenz yelled. "Say it once and for all, for God's sake!"

Suddenly, Old Lorenz gestured to his pistols. Bronco let him go until he practically saw him touching his guns.

"Now!" He said, drawing his own.

Pop Lorenz's revolvers flew through the air. With his wrists bathed in blood, he fell to the ground on his knees.

"Finish it once and for all!" Old Lorenz yelled angrily.

"No ...," Bronco Joe said. "I've waited thirty years for this. To forgive you ..."

He slowly left the town, down the center of Main street.

"He's a man from the West!" Old Parker yelled, raising up his crutch. But Bronco Joe didn't hear him. He was already riding his horse very far away en route to the sweet plains of glory.

And so it happened in Tombstone, Arizona: "The town that refused to die."

At Eleven, Get In on the Action

All of that had happened. He remembered it now alone. He closed his eyes and it was as if he were in the Buck Rogers' Time Warp and landing on the planet of No Return. Where he could change the past at whim. He then remembered the stories piled under his bed. "Witch Tales," "Frontier," "El que la hace la paga," "Superman," "Walt Disney's Stories."

He felt he was leaving Walt Disney behind. Before he had lived for him, and had dreamed of being Gladstone Gander, the lucky one who found diamonds wherever he was. Or Scrooge McDuck, Donald Duck's uncle, who was swimming in millions and ate hot dogs to save ten cents. He liked Scrooge McDuck. He would have liked to be like that.

The owner of the house where he lived was a filthy rich Spaniard who was a lot like Scrooge McDuck. He walked around Santa Fe on Sundays with a cedar walking stick just like Scrooge McDuck's.

"I'm thorry, I'm thorry … I'm thrict about payments. Dear thir, pay me. Fine! I'll wait until Monday."

"Mr. Castelón is a nice guy," Agar commented that day.

Mama Pepita shot him a hard look from the kitchen.

"He's a no-good son-of-a-bitch," she said.

Agar didn't say anything else. He would have liked to have been Castelón's nephew. Uncle Scrooge Castelón, the golden old man who swam in bills from the bank.

He left aside the Disney stories.

Mickey Mouse was still looking for diamonds on the Lost Island.

Gladstone Gander was about to find Tutankhamen's treasure.

Elmer Fudd remained lost under an avalanche in the Himalayas.

He now preferred "Witch's Tales," "The Spirit," "Macabre Stories." Although he knew that at night he would have insomnia and that things would reach for the bottoms of his feet.

He opened the book:

It was the story of Clay Putnam. The man who was hiding a secret. The unknown man who always walked with a box on his shoulder. What was Putnam hiding? The town asked itself. At church, the people would stop praying and turn their eyes on him. Who would pray without taking the box off of his shoulder?

One winter afternoon, Clay Putnam went into Peter's Café. He asked for a glass of gin.

"I'm sorry, Putnam," the barman said. "I won't serve you until you get that damned box off your shoulder."

"Leave me alone!" Putnam yelled. "Leave me alone with my blasted box!"

The men left their drinks and surrounded him.

"What do you have in there, you devil?"

"Show us what you have in that box, you damned warlock!"

"What did you come to Finstown to do, Putnam? Did you maybe come to cast a spell on us?"

Putnam backed away to the door and started running down the street with his box.

"Go after him, get that warlock, even if he's the devil himself!"

Putnam fell to the ground. The men reached him, panting. Old Carson MacCullers raised his wooden stake and brought it down forcefully over his heart. The heart of Clay Horace Putnam, "The Man with the Mysterious Box."

"Open that box!" MacCullers ordered. "Let's get to the bottom of this mystery."

Old Edward Albee leaned over the dead man. An air of expectation surrounded the men.

"Here goes!" Albee yelled, lifting the lid.

"Holy God in heaven above ..."

And the surprised eyes of the inhabitants of Finstown contemplated Putnam's horrible secret: there was another head on his shoulder!

That was Putnam's mystery. "Finstown's Bicephalous Man."

Agar shuddered. The drawing of the other head made quite an impression on him. He was now reading "Vampires in the Belfry" when he sensed the door creaking behind him.

"What are you doing?" Mama Pepita asked roughly. "Why are you shaking? Get to the table!" She said, turning around. "I want you to finish that plate of chickpeas without a single complaint."

At Twelve, an Old Lady Snivels

You went back to your room.

You could also play "The Colors a Blind Man Sees." You cover your eyes and press them tight with your fingers. That's how the pain comes, but you'll see a kaleidoscope of lights and unknown colors. And best of all, a red dot at the center through which you can escape and see yourself from the inside.

Grandma Hazel would tell you that you're going to go blind from so much squeezing, but deep down, the idea doesn't bother you.

To go blind. Marching with a red-tipped walking stick and being protected by everybody. Then Papa Lorenzo wouldn't be able to raise his hand to me and I would eat whatever I wanted and on Sundays I could go to the theater to see this movie or that and ... shit! How would a blind person go to the movies?

So you preferred to stay as you were. Although you remembered the joke: "It was twelve at night and the sun was beating down on the rocks. Under a burnt-out lamp, a blind man read a newspaper without letters."

You started to laugh.

You really were happy alone.

"Ah!" you said. And you thought. And you thought about your penis. Although you didn't take it out because Mama Pepita could come in whenever she wanted and the very thought of such a scene made you die of shame.

Maybe she would say: You disgusting thing! Are these the filthy things you learn in school?

And the word "school" reminded you that vacation would

soon be over and you'd have to see the face of Agrispina Pérez Pérez again, the fifth-grade teacher. Do you remember? That day, she was teaching a class on Descriptive Anatomy.

"This," Agrispina said, "is the kidney. Here are the bladder and the liver. And this is the urinary tract."

And she tapped on the human map with her pinewood pointer.

Henry moved behind you, excited.

"Did you see that?" he whispered. "Agrispina pointed at the balls."

Agrispina continued singing to her class in a soprano voice and walked around the room looking up at the ceiling. On the beach at Santa Fe, they said she didn't have a husband. Was it true? In any event, the West Side Boys said it was, while talking in a circle at recess.

The Boys on one side and the teachers on the other. Both groups talking in low voices and looking at each other with reciprocal loathing.

Sometimes, Agrispina called someone from the group and made him stand up before her. She then turned to the other teachers and said with contempt,

"Look at this one!" And with that, she made a gesture, waving her hand. "You can leave now!"

They hated her. The West Side Boys had even made up a song about her. You remembered it now that you were drawing a naked woman.

Old Agrispina
has never seen a wiener.
Green grass, green grass,
she has a smelly ass.

"The human body is made up of 204 bones, as you all know," she was saying, and then she brought the pointer down on Ulysses' head, a hunched over and silent boy who spent the day drawing Martian spaceships. Then she turned to you and grabbed you tightly by the ear.

"Give me that piece of paper, you little cretin," Agrispina Pérez Pérez said. "Do you think I didn't see the filth you drew?"

You were livid. You stood up and quickly put the drawing in your mouth.

"He swallowed it! He swallowed it!" The voices sang.

"Spit it out!" Agrispina ordered. "Spit it out or I will keep your ear!"

Paper is paper. And notebook paper won't go down a dry throat. You could feel the cartilage in your windpipe.

"Spit it out!"

You let it go. The rolled up ball fell to the floor and she calmly leaned over to pick it up.

"Ha!" She smiled with satisfaction. "How good is this?"

"This time, you can say goodbye, Agar," expectant voices whispered. "They're going to throw you out. They're going to throw you out."

Agrispina adjusted her wire-rim glasses and began to straighten out the saliva-ridden ball of paper on her desk.

To you, it seemed like the Earth was opening up under your feet, and that you were falling, falling, falling into the void again.

"Splendid!" Agrispina exclaimed. "So very illustrative, very illustrative, very ..."

And the bell rang. But you stayed inside. With Agrispina and the smell of the dead classroom.

The difference now. Without the children's sweat. Without the leather of their book bags. From the walls, the patriots again looked at you strictly.

"Swear!" Papa Lorenzo said, suddenly emerging from your memory.

"What's up, Doc!" Bugs Bunny said, hopping around inside your head.

Agrispina looked at you in silence. With the drawing of the naked woman in her hands.

"I would like to know," she said, "what do all of you have in your heads? Do you think that I don't know what you do when you get together in your circle at recess? Make fun of me, that's what you do! And say dirty things and write terrible things about me in the bathroom."

He looked at her, expressionless.

"And now you draw this!"

And she held up the drawing of the woman.

"Who told you that women are like this under their clothes? Tell me! Did your father tell you? Who? I'm waiting … come on!"

This is the island of Cuba, discovered by Columbus. Rodrigo de Triana also came along. What did Columbus do when he first set foot on the island?

"Place the other one behind it, dude. If he hadn't, he would have lost his balance."

Laughter. Laughter. Laughter.

"Names!"

"Who?"

"What's up, Doc!" Bugs Bunny said.

Hardy har har.

71

We were in the West, son ... in the West ... in the W—

You shook your head. You would have liked to turn into an ant. You would have liked to say, *Hickory Dickory Dock, the mouse ran up the clock.*

"Fuck the mouse!" You screamed in your head.

Agrispina slumped down in her desk, overcome by defeat.

"Come on ...," she said, exhausted. "What do the kids say about me? What's that thing they sing?"

Come on ...

Tell me ...

Sing it ...

At Thirteen, a Midget Can Be Seen

At noon, the guys from the Rotary club arrived. They came in a gray truck, with the words "Rotary Club International" inscribed on the door.

Papa Lorenzo went out to meet them in shorts and a T-shirt, and Mama Pepita ran to the bathroom to quickly get herself ready.

"One day they'll take me for the maid," she complained. "A rag is what I am, a rag!"

Agar watched the Rotarians get out of the vehicle with Carnival whistles and shakers.

"The terrible bunch!" Papa Lorenzo greeted them, trying on his best smile.

So they got out: old Mutt Martinez, shortstop for the Santa Fe

Club softball team. The very fat Jeff de la Vega, pitcher. Ambrosio Choraliza, owner of the "La Principal" ball field and supplementary member of the club's board of consultants. Mingo, the barber, "the man who, on the whole beach, knew the most about the Big Leagues," in Papa Lorenzo's words. Ciriaco Sardinas, the Club's Honorary President, who was carrying the Rotarians' bell and banging on it with a hammer, requesting: "Keep this party orderly."

"So what says the old man?" Ambrosio Choraliza greeted him, giving Papa Lorenzo a big hug.

"We've come to take whatever we can get from you, you old joker," Mingo confessed, rubbing his hands with a mischievous expression.

"Order!" Ciriaco Sardinas demanded, hitting the bell. "I won't accept that bit about being a joker. As the club's president, I forbid any such references."

"Damn, people!" Papa Lorenzo said amid the group's laughter. "It looks like you're here to really come down on me."

"Come on, Lorenzo, one day a year, old man …!"

Laughter.

Papa Lorenzo entered the house for a minute and went over to Agar.

"Go to Núñez's house and get him to give you a dozen beers. Get them over here and bring them through the back."

Mama Pepita came out of the bathroom. She had left her tragic air in the mirror and was now smiling broadly.

"Madame!" Mutt greeted her, bowing like a medieval knight.

"Man, it looks like time stands still around here!" Jeff de la Vega commented, looking at Mama Pepita mischievously.

73

"Oh!" She pretended to be embarrassed, going along with his joke. "You really are a joker, Jeff, such a flatterer …"

"Madame, Jeff de la Vega does not flatter, but rather recognizes virtue. That is my motto."

Another flattering phrase.

"Don't bend over too much, old man!" Choraliza warns. "Mind your hinges don't break."

Laughter.

"I'm in great shape!" Jeff shouted amid the guffaws.

"You think?" Mutt said. "The other day, playing softball, you almost ended up hunchbacked forever. We're going to have to drag you along on roller skates, old man!"

Renewed laughter.

"What's wrong, Jeff?" Papa Lorenzo asked, pretending to be serious. "Are you going to let them shoot you down like that?"

"Just ignore them, old man." Jeff said, with an air of resignation. "Today's Sunday."

Agar arrived with the bottles. Papa Lorenzo saw him come in the back door out of the corner of his eye and told Mama Pepita, "Lady, put some music on for us."

"I knew it was worth coming to this house!" Ciriaco Sardinas exclaimed, euphoric.

"Your credit is good here," Papa Lorenzo said.

They drank. Agar watched them through the blinds, exploring their faces and figures and entertaining himself looking for similarities with the characters from all the stories.

"Listen, old man," Ciriaco said. "Yesterday, I was offered a 1954 Studebaker. A gem. A real gem! You know how much?"

"How much?" Papa Lorenzo wanted to know, feigning interest.

Agar watched him pretend and asked himself if the old Rotarians also noticed that his show of interest was all a lie.

"Two and a half!" Ciriaco Sardinas said. "Two and a half, old man."

"I don't believe it," the very fat Jeff de la Vega opined. "Gentlemen, a 1954 Studebaker is, here and in the Belgian Congo, a 1954 Studebaker!"

"Well ... well ...," Ambrosio Choraliza interrupted. "Here comes the sentimental part of the matter." And he pointed at Mama Pepita who was arriving with the tray full of new glasses.

"Ahhh!"

"The anchovies are eavesdropping!" Mingo, the barber, pointed out. "Gentlemen, there's nothing like having a very cold beer and a lot of anchovies to see Warren Span pitch. Gentlemen, it's quite something!"

Agar threw himself down on the bed. He knew that the conversation would now be about baseball for half an hour. And afterwards, Ambrosio Choraliza would talk about something like "the future repairs of the Santa Fe beach gutters." And then things would move on to Ciriaco Sardinas' agenda, who would take that under consideration for the following Monday, at the weekly meeting. He closed his eyes. He knew what would happen afterward. The Rotarians would leave. And Papa Lorenzo and Mama Pepita would go all the way to the gate with them to say goodbye, sending regards to their respective families and kisses to all.

And afterward, Mama Pepita would pick up the bottles, load the tray and take everything to the kitchen. And Papa Lorenzo would stay at the gate for a little while longer, until the Rotarians' truck turned down 12th Street and got lost forever. Then his smile would disappear and he wouldn't let his shoulders slump in defeat.

"Cretins ... ," he would later say. With an old, deep exhaustion.

And Agar would listen from his room to Mama Pepita going through the Trunk of Photos of her Youth, and would hear her say: "this picture was taken when I was fifteen ... was I fifteen or sixteen? Well, in any event, it's all the same."

At Fourteen, an Old Man Is Clean

The Rotarians had left.

From his room, Agar saw Papa Lorenzo come in and drop down on the sofa, in defeat.

The afternoon was clear and suffocating and a dusty drowsiness hung in the air. Papa Lorenzo flipped through the stories in the *National Daily News* and after a while, gave a moribund smile.

Papa Lorenzo is full of mystery. He has two faces, like the bicephalous man from Finstown. Ha, ha, he laughs, and with his other face, he's saying: May a thunderbolt strike you all dead!

Mama Pepita passes on the way to her room.

"Get that look off your face," she said, when she passed by her husband.

He looked at her and said sharply, "I'm very happy! Surely, I have reason to be ..."

"In this house," Mama Pepita said, "it always feels like a funeral."

And she went to her room and Agar heard her shuffling the old photos around.

Silence.

Papa Lorenzo dropped the newspapers and sat staring at a point on the wall. Stunned.

"I know I'm a beast," he admitted then, without addressing anyone. "I can't be any other way. I can't."

He smelled himself under his arms and fell backward on the sofa.

Agar knew what would come now. He knew that Papa Lorenzo would collapse across the sofa, looking vacantly at a point on the wall. Now Papa Lorenzo would write in the air with the tip of his finger. He wrote:

STALIN

"The Man of Steel ...," Papa Lorenzo then murmured. He seemed extremely worn out.

His face, marked with lines, was bitter when he said, "*Comrades! Everyone already knows the story of productive forces and the social relations of production. Everyone knows the law of quantitative and qualitative changes. And everyone knows about the insoluble alliance between the peasants and the proletariat.*"

His voice was dramatic. Theatrical. Agar heard him echoing in the stillness of the living room and thought that if he were Papa Lorenzo's audience, he wouldn't have liked his style of delivering speeches.

Papa Lorenzo leapt from the sofa and returned to his speech, directed at the silent walls: "*A deficient superstructure has a corresponding deficient economic base. The poverty of this society must be sought in the social and material roots of these miserable people. This is an island of cork that floats thanks to the magical illusion of all its components. Ahhhh! But Moctezuma's troops are already dispersed. The flags of the Communist Party are already old. The promised land will not come, nor will the dynamite train. Not hide nor hair of it. Comrades! The revolution needs new vitality! New blood! New faces! This is the truth never revealed. This is the reason of all reasons ..."*

Applause, Agar thought. He peeked through a gap in the door and saw Papa Lorenzo with his arm raised and his finger pointing at the ceiling lamp.

His arm dropped. His finger returned to its natural arrogance. Papa Lorenzo let himself fall down on the sofa again.

"I'm a piece of shit," he said from there. He didn't seem to say it bitterly. He said it with conviction and a bit of resigned indifference. "We are all pieces of shit! You!" he said, turning toward the room where Mama Pepita was going through the old photos. "Me!" he said. "And even that exasperating little kid you gave birth to!"

Agar hid his head under the pillow.

Papa Lorenzo lounged on the sofa and sighed deeply.

"In short ...," he sighed, "all shit."

And he remained quiet, with his gaze lost on the ceiling.

"Aren't you going to keep yelling?" Mama Pepita was pretending not to care: "Keep yelling, you idiot. So the neighbors hear you. Come on, keep yelling!"

"I'll yell whenever I want!" Papa Lorenzo yelled. "I pay for this house with my money!"

Mama Pepita slammed the pictures down and went out to the living room. Agar foresaw the storm and quickly closed the door of his room.

"That boy is listening to all of this," Mama Pepita said. "And outside, they can hear everything as if you were being broadcast on the radio."

Agar closed his eyes slowly. He was returning to absolute darkness and going over his life—his memories came to him in a rush.

"Your father is a very strange communist," Grandma Hazel said. "First, he went around getting votes and organizing strikes and even made me vote for the Popular candidate. And now he became an accountant, and he wants to put you in an elite school, and to hell with strikes, and votes, and I'm still affiliated with that Popular candidacy. Now it turns out he's a Rotary! Communist and International Rotary. I don't understand. *It's a matter of strategy*, he says. Strategy? I don't understand anything about strategy. I want him to give me my voting card back! That's what I want!"

And she stuck her head in the cauldron and scraped the bottom of it with a spatula. She took it out again to say:

"Do you think I don't know that the Communists are going to do away with the home food delivery business if they come to power? Your own father told me so! With Lenin and Stalin's star, they will do away with my food delivery business. No! I am voting against myself! I want him to give me my voting card back! I want to vote for the Authentic Party. And remember this, my son:

"*Long live communism, long live friendship, and if you have two dollars, give me one.*"

And she laughed, surrounded by the smoke from her cauldrons. Like that witch in "Macabre Stories" who flew toward the belfry on a broomstick.

Communist! Agar thought. I don't want my father to be a communist. "The Cobra King" is also a communist and flies in a communist-propelled airplane, and has his base on Red Island, from where he attacks the Black Falcons. Chuck, Olaf, Endrickson,

Stanislaus, André the Frenchman, and Chop Chop the Chinaman.

Holy moly! I'd liked to be in that group. And I'd pass through the circle of West Side Boys with the falcon engraved on my shirt. And Papa Lorenzo would come, without whistling at me, and would ask me in all humility to come back home.

"I'm sorry," I said.

"It will weigh on you," Papa Lorenzo said.

And later he returned in "The Infernal Circle" and tried to pass over us.

"Die, capitalist pigs!" Papa Lorenzo would shout, and our bullets would crash against the tracks of his wheels.

He opened his eyes. Sergeant York appeared on the bathroom wall again. He remembered that he had also fought in the "War Fronts." Like that day on which the two of them were wrapped up in combat smoke.

"Giddy up, kid!" Sergeant York said. He was sweating copiously and crushing a piece of paper in his hand.

"Once and for all, kid—jump! It's the Chinese people who are asking for your help against the Reds."

Agar got ready to jump.

"Wait!" York said. He held onto his shoulder, holding something out to him.

"Take this, kid. It's a five dollar bill. It's a little wrinkled, but still good. When this hell is over, son ... have yourself a tall beer and toast to the health of your old Sergeant York. Will you do it?"

"York!" Agar yelled."Sergeant York!"

York had died.

Agar looked at the battlefield and understood that the battle was being decided there, at that exact moment. And, without thinking about it, he threw himself furiously on the enemy. On the red Chinese and the yellow men from Korea.

No. He definitely did not like Communists.

The falcon, Sergeant York and all the others were handsome, and the Communists are bald and toothless.

"All of them with their asses patched up," Grandma Hazel would say. "All of them smelling like a bike shop."

At Fifteen, I'll Get Your Spleen

The afternoon went by. In his room, he felt the heavy air, weighed down with drowsiness.

The afternoon went by and he had spent almost the whole day punished. Summer vacation was going by and he had spent almost his entire vacation being punished.

He would have given his right hand to go outside. He would have placed it on Odin's pyre and would have said to the God of the Vikings:

"Burn! But let me out."

He peeked through the door jamb. On the sofa, Papa Lorenzo was writing a long speech in the air. He thought he could ask for his permission. Although later he thought that if he asked him, Papa Lorenzo could turn his back to him and pretend he was asleep. Or he may just say:

"Go ask your mother!"

And then he'd go to Mama Pepita and she'd say:

"Me? Go ask your father!"

And so he would go in circles from one side to the other until he burst out crying in rage.

Nonetheless, his Interior Voice suggested this time:

"Ask him for it ... what do you have to lose?"

"I could end up with a mule kick," he reconsidered.

So he decided to appeal to Imaginary Fate and conceived of the formula to make a decision once and for all.

Papa Lorenzo was writing in the air with his back to him. If he turned around, he would give him what he asked for.

He waited.

He waited.

He waited.

Papa Lorenzo started turning around slowly. Agar's heart beat quickly.

He reached the sofa. Papa Lorenzo picked the newspaper off the floor and opened it again to the comic pages.

"I'm going to the movies," Agar stammered.

Papa Lorenzo commented:

"Did Little Orphan Annie die after all?"

"I'm going to the movies ..."

"What's that?" Papa Lorenzo pretended to listen for the first time.

"I'm going to the movies," Agar repeated.

"If you have the money, I'm not opposed," Papa Lorenzo said.

"Papa, everyone is going to the movies today. They're showing a Red Ryder film."

"There's no money," Papa Lorenzo said without looking up from his newspaper.

Agar knew he was running a risk if he persisted. Nonetheless, he tried again: "Papa … don't you have seventy cents? That's all a movie costs."

Papa Lorenzo looked at him, irritated. Then he turned around on the sofa, showing him his back.

"Don't go …," he said from there. "The Siboney Indians never went to the movies, and they were happy."

Mama Pepita dropped the pots and pans and came out of the kitchen.

"You're a monster!" She yelled. "Your answer to everything is the Indians. I haven't worn a new dress for five years, simply because the Indians walked around naked—and they were happy! And for six months I've been walking around with this horrible rat's nest on my head, simply because the Indians didn't get permanents—and they were happy! Everything goes back to the Indians. But the Indians are kaput!"

She was yelling.

Papa Lorenzo, his face buried in the back of the sofa, pretended he was asleep. In the end, he opened his eyes, feigned a TV commercial smile, and said: "There's no money."

Mama Pepita grumbled again and began to circle the sofa, looking for Papa Lorenzo's eyes to throw his indolence in his face. She finally managed to irritate him. So Papa Lorenzo leapt from the sofa and ran around the room and started to turn everything over shrieking:

"THERE ISN'T ANY!"

And then, he pulled the drawers from the closet, and started to empty the Closet of Souvenirs, screaming:

"THERE ISN'T ANY!" and throwing Bukharin and Kropotkin's books.

"THERE ISN'T ANY!" he said, throwing Stalin's photos against the walls.

"THERE ISN'T ANY!" he said, tossing up the old communist newspapers.

"THERE ISN'T ANY. THERE ISN'T ANY. THERE ISN'T ANY. THERE ISN'T ANY!"

And at last exhausted, he fell over the mess of clothing and red books, huffing.

"I'm disgusted," Papa Lorenzo then said. "My life is a real son of a bitch."

At Sixteen, Run from that Ox So Lean!

Agar took advantage of the confusion and slipped out to the yard; Papa Lorenzo's screams could still be heard from inside the house. He lay down at last, behind Mama Pepita's wash tub. From there, he contemplated an incredibly blue sky with some incredibly white clouds.

I'll play the cloud game, he thought.

It wasn't hard for him to find Sergeant York, with his helmet and backpack, firing from the sky.

The cloud, in its turtle-pace path, fell apart and later became an angry Apache. And then it became Tonka: the wild horse. And later it was a spider in a circle of rocks. In the end, it took on the shape of a large rabbit. It was Bugs Bunny, "the Lucky Wabbit."

"So long, folks!" Bugs Bunny said, lifting a hand made of white smoke. "We're going to the land of giant carrots …"

84

Papa Lorenzo went by too, followed by Agrispina Pérez Pérez and the witch from "Macabre Stories" and the bicephalous man from Finstown.

He caressed his penis. Now he could take it out without any problem. There, at the end of the yard, Mama Pepita would never be able to surprise him and he would be able to put it away before she could see him.

So he took it, definitively, in his hands, and rubbed it like a good Boy Scout rubs a pine stick to make a fire in the dark forest.

He was just playing.

Because he never felt that ticklish sensation that Tin Marbán mentioned.

He was like that for a while, rubbing himself as he reviewed the clouds, absorbed. Discovering in them new faces, objects and characters that took shape in their slow march toward the West. He closed his eyes.

The great star Tongolele, who announced Sensat oil, found him in his boudoir.

"Hello!" she exclaimed, disconcerted. "Were you here?"

Quasimodo saw her lift her leg and undo her garter straps. She was then barefoot on the rug, and walked around the room, with her zipper down.

She turned toward Quasimodo then, and with an air of indifference, she took off her bra. Quasimodo contemplated her tits shaking freely and threw himself on them.

"What are you doing, you monster!"

He trapped her between his hands. He could feel his heart beating at the tip of his phallus. His gigantic, eighteen inch phallus.

Tongolele fell, definitively conquered, onto the grass of his boudoir. Quasimodo violently entered that soft body, listening to the crunching of membranes and the squealing of organs. Tongolele's organs, the great star of Sensat Oil. The woman with the fabulous tits who—

Suddenly, he shuddered.

Inside his head came an unexpected somersault.

He felt that something inside him was coming loose.

Something was being unleashed after having been shut up for thousands of years. New. Unknown. Something that shook him to the marrow of his bones and caused strong shudders of pleasure.

Something had erupted from his deepest insides. And now in a grandiose stupor, he looked at his hands.

Thick, white lava.

Sticky lava like the saliva from a cold.

Like paste itself.

He understood everything at once during that decisive moment. With an unfamiliar calm, he stood up and went to the gate of the yard.

Then he said, solemnly and seriously: *Ladies and Gentlemen.*

As if before the Grand Jury of Public Opinion.

And he started running forever.

The sun was beating down hard on the wild rosemary, and its rays were melting over the countryside in purple and greenish lights. And from a wall, a lizard took out its red tie in the intermittent signal of "danger," "danger," "danger."

HAVANA, 1968

THE MAGIC STILL

THE DEVIL AND THE NUN

They called her La Baudilia, because she was the exact female version of her brother, that famous Baudilio Cartablanca, who later ended a long career as a Venezuelan revolutionary, dying a renegade. She had the same sharp nose, the same bulging eyes, and the same measured and gentle way of speaking that hid, or tried to hide, a naive self-sufficiency.

I met her at the Quintelas' home, in the Apolo neighborhood, and I quickly hit it off with her because of her open and aggressive spirit, and the fact that she was a great storyteller.

One of those stories was about her own life.

She said she had come to know love late in life because, as a girl, her brother scared off her boyfriends. She said it with a smile, although with a distant note of bitterness. The last of her suitors was a young man, Consolación, from her town, who dressed very elegantly, and always showed up with a handful of roses, smelling of French cologne. He seemed like one of the knights of old. His relationship with her did not go beyond an inoffensive clutching of hands and a whispering exchange of songs. Their courtship lasted three months, until the day on which Baudilio, her ferocious brother, came home early from a political meeting and confronted the young man with a disdainful expression.

The suitor was a refined young man. He crossed his legs in the English manner and spoke with the voice of a provincial poet. Baudilio looked him over, found out he was a symbolist poet, touched the feeble muscles of his arm, and at last said mockingly, "So this is the little fag you found for yourself."

It was the end. The young man wanted to protest, but he couldn't. Instead of daring to respond to the insolence with a strong word or a punch in the mouth, he left the house in shame, tears in his eyes, and never returned.

"Right there, I decided to become a nun."

She decided it in silence, counting on her Roman Catholic and Apostolic mother's complicity. First, she was put in a convent on Calle 23, in the heart of Havana that didn't let in sunlight or even the sound of swallows chirping.

Her brother Baudilio went there with four drunk friends to rescue her and bring her back to the outside world. But the nuns refused to open the doors; they didn't let him see her, and everything ended when her brother, sauced with rum, unloaded the cartridge of a machine gun on the convent's old wall and left, cursing the priests and swearing he would return one day to remove her by force.

Perhaps that was why the convent's superior decided to send La Baudilia to Madrid, to a convent on San Cosme and San

Damián Street, where they worked hard and only spoke of essential matters. That was where La Baudilia's crisis of conscience began. Why was she there? Why should she hand her life over to God in such an absurd way? She endured some very agonizing days due to the immensity of her doubts. She even doubted Saint Teresa, who was her inspiration on dark nights. On one of those nights, she couldn't take it anymore and went to the convent's altar, seeking an answer.

The altar was dark, only a small candle at the feet of a plaster Saint Teresa shed a little light.

La Baudilia fell in desperation before Christ on the cross and said:

"Lord, take pity on me. If you are real, if you exist, show yourself right now and give me the strength to follow this path."

But God did not show himself, nor was his voice heard, nor did any light flicker strangely.

Then she turned toward the darkest part of the chapel and spoke thus:

"Satan, I am not afraid of you. If you truly exist, turn yourself into flesh and blood so I can see you and be your eternal servant."

But the devil didn't appear either. Nothing.

The next day, she packed her belongings, dressed in lay clothes, and went straight to the airport to return to Cuba, to her brother, and to the revolution.

That was her story.

"None of it exists," she said to us, at last, leaning against the front door. "God, the devil, it's all a lie."

And she left. Rosa and I leaned out the window to see her walk off down Calle Mariel. She was wearing men's jeans, a Caribbean cruise shirt that was too large for her, electrician boots, a hairstyle like a cocky Frenchman, and her gait was aggressive and shameless like a tough guy from the Pogolotti neighborhood.

Then, the Quintelas and I looked down at our hands in silence, looked in each other's faces again in silence, and understood, in silence, how terrible it was. How terribly and expertly the devil worked.

AN AXE TO THE SIDEBURNS

The door to Alipio's barbershop opened first thing in the morning and a man with a thug-like face entered, dressed in a blue security guard uniform with a holster full of bullets from which hung a Star handgun in its case. Alipio saw him arrive and felt a chill rise up through his legs and take root in his heart, which skipped a beat.

It was him. Alipio had not forgotten that ocher-colored face, the hairy ears, the gold tooth, the thin mustache that had been so in vogue back in the 1950s. It was him. Thirty years was not enough to change his basic characteristics. It was him. Here, in Miami, he was the security guard of some cemetery or clothing store; over there, in Cuba, before the revolution, he was Captain Ovidio Samá of the Military Intelligence Service with an evil, ferocious, and mean reputation.

For the first time in a long time, Alipio thought again about his son. He would have been forty-eight years old, and with the gift he'd had for numbers, he would perhaps now be an excellent economist or a brilliant accountant. That was what he was studying at the University when they killed him. Accounting.

"Do you want to sit down?" Alipio asked. "There's another barber, but he gets here at ten."

"I just came for a shave." The man said in a raspy voice that matched his looks.

"Then sit down. I'll be with you right away."

The man sat down in Alipio's chair and closed his eyes as if he were about to sleep.

"Do you want a very close shave?"

"Yes."

Alipio took his razor and began to sweep it along his leather apron. He had spent many years looking for this man who he now had in his hands. He had gone to Jacksonville because they told him he lived there. Later, they told him he was in New Jersey, but there, they told him he had gone to Kansas to be a nightclub security guard. He ran around Kansas with a gun and a long sharp Sevillana knife. He visited every bar, pool hall, and seedy den, asking about that damned Ovidio Samá who in 1957 had killed his son during a university protest. Later, he stopped looking for him, since the latest reports said he was drug trafficking in Venezuela.

But now, fate placed Samá in his hands. A son. His only child. What he had most loved in his life. And this abominable man had emptied a machine gun into his son's body, leaving him almost unrecognizable.

"Do you want me to clear out your blackheads?"

94

"Don't worry about that. I just want a shave."

"Has it been a long time since you came over?"

"Almost thirty years," he replied. "I was one of the first ones to leave. How about you?"

"I came later." Alipio said. "I believed in it at the beginning, but later became disillusioned."

"That happened to a lot of people."

They didn't talk anymore. Alipio applied the shaving cream, brushed it on, and with his razor in hand began to outline the right side burn. This would be the right time. A little bit of pressure in his arm and that head would fall lifeless over the white sheet. But, then what? No one would believe it was an accident. No one would understand that revenge that had lasted for thirty years. Alipio swept the razor clean across the man's right cheek, then he noticed a cyst on his chin and it took all his self-control to avoid it.

The man remained silent, with his eyes closed, as if intensely enjoying the coolness of the cream and the pleasant cutting of the razor. From now on, any moment was right for Alipio. Thirty years. Thirty years. He moved to the other cheek and shaved him in three precise motions.

"Your mustache, do you want it like that or shorter?"

"It's fine like that," the man said. "I've always worn my mustache like Clark Gable."

Nonetheless, Alipio took the scissors and cut some hairs from the mustache and the nose, in addition to trimming the customers' bushy eyebrows. He couldn't. Now he realized that he couldn't. No one would understand his story. He would spend the rest of his life in jail and, worse still, he would see the blood run, albeit the blood of a thug, but blood that would be weighed just the same when the time came in Heaven for a final account of his life.

Alipio finished. He dried the man's face with a clean towel and removed the sheet from his chest. Then he held out a mirror and the man looked at himself for a few seconds.

"Satisfied?"

"More or less," the thug said.

"That's three dollars."

The man took out a wallet and removed a five dollar bill.

"Keep the change," he said.

"Thank you," Alipio mumbled, a shadow falling over his face.

The man went over to the barbershop's big mirror and adjusted his shirt collar and tie. Then he said: "I came here because they told me you wanted to find me and kill me. But now you realize it's not so easy to kill."

THE ILLUSTRATED WOMAN

Taking license with Ray Bradbury

If you ever pass through Citrus Park, I recommend that you not enter Miss Roberta Donovan's bar. Keep going, at full speed, and try not to listen to the siren's song of the women tattooed on that enormous madam. I had the bad luck of stopping in Citrus because my car broke down there. The radiator, the spark plugs, who knows what went wrong with my old '69 Mazda. Today it's gone forever in the sands of that ghost town.

Because, gentlemen, Citrus Park is a ghostly town. There are no garages, no markets, no pharmacies, no cafés: nothing. One glance is enough to understand that it's completely uninhabited, perhaps due to those hurricanes in the early part of the century that beat the Florida coast with unusual fury. The houses are in ruins, the streets are made of white sand, and millions of giant red ants crawl over everything in search of scarce shrubs found around the periphery. They're enormous ants, perhaps

97

the world's largest, and they attack humans, leaving enormous terribly itchy welts.

But that's where I ended up. Woodland, the closest town, is eighteen miles away, and I was too tired to make the journey by foot. So I decided to spend the night there, in Citrus Park, and to leave for Woodland first thing in the morning. The heat made me take off my shirt, and curiosity led me to wander the streets of that sad town, in search of a human face. I called out among the uninhabited houses, and then I pissed in the middle of the street, but no one showed up to reprimand me. All I saw was a red lightbulb go on. A solitary red lightbulb in the door of a crumbling bar, whose window announced Coors beer.

I wish I had never entered. I've gone through some difficult moments in my life, but none like that adventure in Donovan's bar. I pushed the door open and went inside. There, the sand from the hurricanes covered the counter and the tables, and the giant ants sought out ivy and purslane to satiate their hunger. There also was the very fat Roberta Donovan, bending over the counter near the cash register that didn't seem to have worked since the 1930s.

Behind the counter was a round stage with a microphone in the center, and on a corner of the curtain hung a sign that read: "Sex at Six." I asked for a Budweiser.

"Hot or cold?" the fat woman asked me in a languorous voice.

"Cold, of course."

"It's a matter of taste. Some people prefer it hot because it has a different effect."

"Give it to me cold."

The fat woman opened the fridge and rummaged around

amid bottles and cans, and after much searching placed a beer right in front of me.

"Are you thinking of staying around here long?" she asked.

"Until tomorrow. First thing, I'm on my way to Miami."

"Then you'll have time to see the show."

"What kind of show?"

"Ladies. The most exciting and most shapely ladies of any bar in the country."

"Where are they?" I wanted to know.

"Here, with me. You'll see them soon."

We didn't talk anymore. I drank a Miller, a Coors, and another Budweiser. It was a quarter to six when fat Donovan served me a last beer. Then she disappeared behind the red curtains.

Citrus Park. How is it possible for someone to live in such a place? That fat woman Donovan had to be either crazy or completely antisocial. How did she feed herself? What food did she eat to maintain that 300-pound body?

I pondered this mystery, until she reappeared before me dressed in a sequin-covered pink cape.

"You want to know what I eat, right?" she said, leaning over the counter again: "well, this."

And she picked up three or four giant ants with her fingers and brought them to her mouth, then chewed them with great pleasure.

"At first, it takes work, but then they end up tasting as delicious as pork rinds. What time is it?"

"Six," I informed her.

"Well, keep your eyes on the show, it's the most unique show on the entire American continent."

She went over to the stage and put on a record by Barry White and his Love Unlimited Orchestra. Little by little, she began swaying her hips slowly while undoing the pink cape button by button.

She ended up naked, and yet there was not an inch on that colossal body that wasn't tattooed. Tattoos of naked women that seemed to move lasciviously to the beat of the slow and exciting music. I thought they were moving as a result of my incipient drunkenness, but when I took a good look, I noticed they were moving on their own, with their own lives, showing their asses, ardently kissing each other, rolling around in twos all over Ms. Donovan's monumental body. It was a lesbian orgy. One of them was whipping another with a riding crop, while another practiced cunnilingus on a blonde with exuberant breasts. Others kissed passionately, united at the pubis.

I was perplexed—even more, I was turned on to the point that my penis wanted to break through my underwear. Suddenly, fat Donovan turned off the turntable. She came over to me slowly, and confidently taking me by the hand, led me to a small room behind the curtains. There, she fell on me like a lustful elephant. But I wasn't looking at her, all of my attention was fixed on the dozens of tattooed women, who kept rolling around with each other, showing off their perfect asses, their divine breasts, their monumental legs. Thus, watching that overwhelming show of hot lesbians, I made love to the very fat Donovan. How many times? Two, three, five; until the tattooed women began to stay still, as if sleeping, and fat Donovan, beyond all tiredness, also fell asleep on top of me. Carefully, I wriggled out from under the weight of her body until I was completely free. Then, an enormous exhaustion came over me, and I fell asleep next to her, facing her enormous back.

I slept very little, it's true, because the giant ants were attacking my feet with canine fury. At two in the morning, I opened my eyes and noticed that fat Donovan was still sleeping and snoring, despite the giant ants. Her back, her enormous sumo wrestler's back, was the only place on her body without any tattoos. I looked at her white back as if into a mirror for a long time, and little by little, I noticed figures start to appear that had not been in the show. One of them was me in the room, naked and sprawled out asleep, and the other one was fat Donovan, who with a sickle was chopping off my penis all in one stroke.

I sprang quickly from the bed. Very carefully, I put on my pants and shoes. I left the room on tip toe and headed quickly to the wide intercoastal highway that would lead me to Miami.

I quickened my pace. My heart pounded. There, in the distance, I could see the lights of a town. Woodland, maybe. Or perhaps Alexandria. I didn't know, the only thing I knew for sure was that I had to be in that town, or any town, by break of day.

O PYTHAGORAS!

My first job with Ramses, the photographer of the great beyond, was in steamy Miami Beach, at the Colony Hotel, where every Friday old classicists met who worshipped the ancient philosopher Pythagoras. They wanted Ramses to go there with his prodigious camera because they were going to invoke Pythagoras's presence that day and it would be a good occasion to photograph him should he deign to appear. Ramses would handle the camera, I would take care of the lights, and Luisa, the medium, would try to communicate with Pythagoras from the fourth dimension.

When we arrived at the Colony, the classicists welcomed us with great displays of enthusiasm. They called Ramses "Maestro," his prodigious camera "A Prodigy of the Ages" and they acclaimed the medium as gifted, touched by God's hand.

We entered the lobby and the first thing that stood out were the many different animals there. There were doves, cranes, quails, a cricket, squirrels, white mice, and even an enormous peacock who smugly strutted around the place with its beautiful tail open like a fan.

Mr. Grigorakis, the hotel owner and a tried and true classicist, took us to the wide patio that overlooked the sea, where interested musicians had been playing lyres and singing sweet litanies invoking Pythagoras since seven that morning.

Luisa, the medium, who had been accompanying Ramses since he'd started his business, sat down in a chair in the middle of the circle of happy old men who were singing along to the sound of the lyres.

"Why are there so many animals?" I asked Grigorakis, pulling him aside.

"Because they understand Pythagoras," was his response. And he then explained that, according to Pythagoras, after humans die they inhabit a variety of animals until they go through the entire universe of fauna. Then they again became human beings.

At that moment, Luisa, the medium, shuddered in her chair and fell into a trance, possessed by a spirit.

"I am Pythagoras of Croton," she said in a guttural voice, "and I've been a lion, a chimpanzee, an elephant, an eagle, and a buffalo on the American plains. But today I appear in the body of a man, because my reincarnation cycle has reached its end. Is there love here?"

As their only response, the classicists took each other's hands and started to kiss each other on the lips and the cheeks and to dance around the medium, to the sound of the lyres.

In the meantime, Ramses placed the camera in front of the medium and proceeded to take photos with the lightbulb and electrical-cable-laden device.

The classicists stopped dancing and crowded around the medium, who continued with closed eyes, imprisoned by a series of strong shudders.

Twelve photos were taken, until the medium stood up and said in a masculine voice:

"That's enough for today. I have important missions to carry out in other parts of the world. But you can count on my eternal love, and call me whenever you need me. Ah! And don't forget mathematics. Remember that mathematics is the primal science. And all other branches of knowledge stem from it."

With that, Pythagoras abandoned the medium's body and she fell to the floor face-down, where she lay for a long while, only recovering her senses little by little.

Grigorakis, the leader of the classicists, approached Ramses and asked him if he had managed to see Pythagoras through the lens.

"Just like I see you now," Ramses responded.

"So, when will those photos be ready?" Grigorakis wanted to know.

"You'll have them in your hands on Friday."

"If Pythagoras isn't in them, I'll pay you anyway, but if Pythagoras appears in them, I'll write you a check for six thousand dollars."

"Don't worry," Ramses said, "Pythagoras has been photographed."

They bid us farewell with a lot of applause and blessings and soon we were back on Flagler and 14th Avenue, where Ramses had his studio.

He started to develop the photos right away. I was also there, in the dark room, watching how Ramses developed the negatives under the faint red light. He developed all of them, and then he took a hold of the printing machine and started to print the photos. There appeared the happy old men, the lyre players, Grigorakis on his knees with his arms lifted high, as well as the medium with her eyes closed, surrounded by solemn old men holding each other's hands. But Pythagoras was not there.

"Go find me a picture of Pythagoras in the archive," Ramses ordered me, his voice urgent.

"That's impossible," I told him. "Pythagoras of Croton was never photographed in his lifetime or painted by any artist."

"Well, then look through films set in antiquity for some old, bearded man who looks like a prophet."

I went out to the archive and was looking for what Ramses requested for a long time. In the end, I came upon a photo of John Houston dressed as an ancient Greek, holding a staff in his hand.

I quickly took it to Ramses and asked him if that was what he wanted.

"I like it," he said. "Find me more—seated, standing, talking."

I went back to the archive and was actually able to gather several photos of John Houston in different positions in his prophet garb.

"Perfect," Ramses said with the material in his hands. "Now leave me alone. For this work I need a lot of concentration and solitude."

Ramses spent the whole day working in the dark room. It got

to be five p.m., and the medium and I left the place, with him inside, concentrating on his work.

The next day, when I appeared before him in the dark room, he turned on the lights and showed me his work, still in the dryer.

There you could see the thirty old classicists in Miami Beach surrounding a Pythagoras dressed in a Grecian tunic, raising his staff very solemnly. There were four photos like that. The others were simple views of the hotel and of the jolly old men who radiated happiness as they danced.

"As you see, it's all a trick," Ramses said with a smile. "Pythagoras of Croton never existed, and if he did exist, he must now be old dust over the hot earth of Croton."

"So you don't believe?" I asked him.

"In anything." Ramses responded. "When I left Cuba, I stopped believing in all religion and all philosophy. I embraced money as my ideology."

"But then, this is a scam." I said.

"Perhaps," Ramses responded, looking down at his nails philosophically. "But they're going to be happy with these photos. Their devotion to Pythagoras will lead them to blindly believe that John Houston is the real Pythagoras. They will never suspect that it's a crude photomontage. They'll be happy; I'll have six-thousand dollars in my pocket. What you call a scam, I call a white lie, a dream machine. The camera I have is just a Japanese Nikon to take pictures of weddings and baptisms. Everything decorating it is pure useless junk to create an ambience. So, what do you make of all of this?"

By way of response, I started laughing.

"The perfect business." I said.

"Good," Ramses said. "Now you have to go to Kendall, to 122nd Avenue, to hand over twelve photos to an old woman who lost her daughter three months ago and is obsessed with the idea that the deceased is still living in her house. As you'll notice, the daughter is none other than Bette Davis in the movie "Jezebel," dressed as a late 19th-century lady. If the old lady complains that this isn't her daughter, you'll be able to tell her that spirits change their appearance according to their tastes and, to wander about in the fourth dimension they take on the face they like most. Got it?"

"Got it."

"So go. There are twelve photos and the old lady should give you five hundred dollars, as per the contract. Do you understand?"

"Of course."

"So get going!"

I left the studio in Ramses' car and was soon in Kendall looking for the old woman's home. It took me a while to find the house—it was tucked away, protected by two gates, and guarded by an aggressive Doberman who barked frantically at me from the moment I got out of my car. I rang the doorbell and the old woman answered, leaning on two crutches.

"I've come from Ramses Photos," I said with a forced smile. "I brought the photos the Maestro took of you and your deceased daughter two months ago."

"God bless you, son! I am willing to stop eating for a whole month for those photos. I'll pay any price, but let me see them right away."

I handed over the sealed envelope and she opened it very delicately.

There, in the first photo, you could see the old woman sitting in a gray armchair with Bette Davis behind her, her hands on the old woman's shoulders, dressed in a very elegant suit from the mid-1800s.

"My daughter! My daughter!" the little old woman exclaimed, tears in her eyes. "Why does she look so different? She was thinner."

"Well, spirits take on the form they always wished they'd had in their material lives," I said, evoking Ramses' words. "Believe me, this is the actual appearance your daughter has in the great beyond."

"It doesn't matter," the old woman said. "It doesn't matter to me at all. It's my daughter and I'll pay anything to have her with me again. Do you know how she died?"

"No."

"It's better if you don't know. She was raped eleven times by three criminals, who afterward knifed her repeatedly, and then took everything she had in her purse. She was finishing up veterinary school—at the height of her youth."

"She's happy now with you," I assured her.

"God bless you, son. I won't eat, I won't buy that plot of land in the cemetery I'm saving for. But it doesn't matter. It doesn't even matter to me to go without my heart medicine this month. My little daughter, my dear girl is with me."

She turned around with the photos in her hands and came back a little while later with four one-hundred-dollar bills, all wet and wrinkled.

"Here you go," she said. "That's all I have. I know I'm one hundred dollars short, but I hope to God that kind-hearted Ramses can understand that there just isn't anymore."

"He'll understand," I said. "Don't worry about that."

I shook her bony hand and she gave me a kiss on the cheek.

"You don't know how happy I am now," was the last thing I heard her say when I was already in the car. I bid her farewell with a wave of my hand and went quickly back to the studio on Flagler Street.

"How did it go?" Ramses asked when he saw me.

"Fine. Here's the money."

"Only four hundred? I told her five hundred."

"She doesn't even have a bucket to kick when the time comes," I explained.

"Nonsense! Those old folks have a lot of gold saved in the bank. You should have bargained. Tomorrow, I'll go myself to get that hundred dollars. Now, go to the archive and look for a dachshund. It's for another old lady who can't be consoled after the death of her pet. I already photographed her, all I need is the dog lying at her feet."

Calmly, without any emotion or desire to argue, I said to Ramses, "No, my friend. I'm done with this job right now."

"What's wrong with you, *cubano*? Aren't you happy with the salary you've got? I'll raise it to five hundred dollars a month soon."

"I'm sorry, Ramses, it's not that. Keep the money you owe me. Find someone else to deal with your archive. I'm leaving."

"Oh, I get it. Scruples?"

"Something like that."

"How long have you been in exile?"

"Three months," I responded.

"You'll never get a leg up."

"I know."

"Fine, leave if you want. Take this hundred dollars, you'll need it."

"No, I don't need it. Thank you."

I turned my back to him and walked to the front door. From there, I heard Ramses raise his voice to say to me once more:

"You'll never get a leg up here!"

I went out to the street. It was a beautiful summer afternoon and I started to walk toward downtown. I crossed the bridge, passed in front of the library, walked in front of the showy clothing and jewelry shops, and ended up at a lonesome park that bordered the sea.

There, I threw myself on the sand and leaned my head against a coconut tree. I didn't have even one cent. I didn't know where I was going to sleep in the days that followed, but I felt light, calm, almost happy.

O Pythagoras, Pythagoras! Keep me in mind when we see each other's faces, there, in the afterlife.

THE PHANTOM BUNKER

Ferryman, oh, ferryman. Everything began because of that damned ferryman who was asking three thousand pesos to clandestinely take him out of the country.

"Three thousand, not one peso less," the ferryman said, seated on the porch of his house, leaning against a wall decorated with revolutionary slogans, along with a picture of the tyrant Cornelio Rojas.

In his frustration, Danilo Castellanos had time to once again ponder the farce of a life that all of the country's inhabitants lead. Nobody loved Cornelio Rojas, but in every house, like the ferryman's, there were walls covered with revolutionary slogans and pictures of the dictator in a hundred different positions, in addition to a sign on every door that said, in brilliant letters, "This is your home, Cornelio."

The ferryman, the man who had clandestinely taken more

than five hundred people out on his shark fishing boat, gave the impression of being a loyal soldier to the dictatorship and the tyrant's greatest admirer. "Three thousand, not one peso less," the ferryman said again. And Danilo turned toward the street leading to the port, patting the paltry sixty pesos he had in his pocket. Three thousand; he needed three thousand. To wander the cafés of Paris, to get to know New York, to visit the Prado Museum in Madrid; to live like a free man for the first time in the thirty years he'd been alive. He walked toward the city. On every corner were enormous billboards with Cornelio Rojas's face or those of the leading people in his government. Three thousand, three thousand. A legal ticket on an airplane would've cost a lot less, but Cornelio Rojas had forbidden all men under fifty years of age from leaving the country, due to military strategy and the agricultural need for strong arms and backs. Three thousand. Three thousand. Danilo sat down on a wall, in front of the sea, and began to sadly ponder ways to come up with three thousand pesos. His friends, teachers, and office workers lived day-to-day, like him, spending their paltry salaries on articles sold on the black market. His mother and father had died a long time ago. There was only his aunt Benigna, the aristocrat.

"Benigna is rich," his mother had said to him before dying. "She must have over 20,000 pesos hidden away. But don't ask her for one cent—don't even try. She is the cheapest woman on earth." And his mother added, "she doesn't even keep the money in a bank. She hides it herself in the bathroom of her house, inside the wall, behind a blue tile below the sink."

Aunt Benigna. She was the answer. He would go to her house in the neighborhood of Los Molinos, and he would cry, he would beg, he would kiss her feet so that she would lend him the money.

"None of that will do any good," his mother had said. "My sister Benigna has a heart of steel. She could see you dying of hunger and still be incapable of feeling moved to give you one cent."

Danilo Castellanos looked at the horizon over the sea for a long time. A ship with the French flag passed slowly before him with its prow headed toward freedom. He would steal. He would go see his aunt Benigna and would steal from her without hesitation the three-thousand pesos that the Ferryman required. Just three thousand; that way perhaps his aunt wouldn't immediately notice it was missing. Yes, he would steal, and like the honest man he was, he would quickly return the money as soon as he was in the land of freedom. He stood up on the wall, contemplated the red ball of the sun that was sinking slowly into the sea, filled his lungs with salty air, and walked down the street toward the neighborhood of Los Molinos, one of the city's most exclusive.

As he walked quickly, he pondered the steps he should take. His aunt would be surprised by the visit, after so many years without any word from him. But he would justify his absence by saying he was working as a history teacher in a town out in the countryside. He would smile, hug her, take her that orchid that bloomed in the funeral home's garden. Then the difficult part would come; listening to his aunt, listening to the idiotic things she would say, and going through the enormous family album with her, containing all the photos of the grandparents, cousins, and childhood friends who were now dead or in exile. Then the crucial moment would come; the excuse for going to the bathroom. Diarrhea. That's what he would say. He would feign strong stomach cramps and would ask the old lady if he could use her bathroom. There, below the sink, was the fortune. Three thousand. Just three thousand. And perhaps that same night, he would be on the Ferryman's vessel, covered by a sheet, headed toward international waters, where a Swedish cargo ship or an American cutter or a Canadian cruise ship would take him to the land of freedom.

When he passed in front of the funeral home, he plucked the showy orchid. Then he climbed up the steep street that marked the edges of the exclusive neighborhood of Los Molinos, where the majority of the highest-ranking government officials lived. It was almost night already when he arrived at the three-story building where his aunt Benigna lived. There, more than anywhere else, the streets were full of red flags and the houses displayed full-color pictures of Cornelio Rojas with the slogan that had been read and heard a thousand times: Education, Production, Defense.

Danilo Castellanos took a deep breath before going up the stairs that would take him to the third floor. He wasn't a criminal; he had never stolen and, until then, he had been a dignified history teacher, respected for his moral inscrutability and his far-reaching knowledge of Ancient Greece. But he had to escape. He had become so disenchanted with Cornelio Rojas's revolution that he had a duodenal ulcer and a nervous tic in his eye, which made him especially insecure in front of women. He had to act. Caesar did far more to gain power. Without hesitation, he skipped up the forty steps and as if he were in a movie, saw himself knocking at the door marked number thirty-three, where the shameful sign also hung, announcing, "This is your home, Cornelio." He didn't have to wait long. From the other side of the door, came the voice of an old woman asking, "Who is it?"

And Danilo, waving the orchid, responded in an incredibly

firm voice, "It's me, auntie, your nephew Danilo." A few tense seconds of waiting passed, and then the door opened slowly, allowing the old woman to show her mistrustful eye and study the visitor's appearance. The yelling came right away, "Lord in Heaven above! Kid, it's you! I haven't seen you for years!"

The door opened completely and Danilo melted into a hug with that feeble body that smelled of castor oil and he felt a long, cold kiss on his ear that turned his stomach. She was ugly, wearing a house dress buttoned up to the neck and the skin of her arms and face appeared to be made of onion peel.

"Lord in Heaven above! Lord in Heaven above!"

"Aunt, auntie, you're looking so well!"

"I'm an old lady about to kick the bucket. But you, son, you've become a man. The last time I saw you was at your mother's wake."

"I remember."

"You've let me down, Danilo. You don't even visit on my birthday. I bet you've forgotten the date on which your poor aunt was born."

"Honestly, yes I have, auntie. But I haven't completely forgotten you. I still remember how much you like orchids, and I bought you this one at the cemetery flower shop."

"It's so beautiful! I'll put it in the refrigerator with some aspirin so it lasts several weeks."

She turned around with the orchid in hand and Danilo had time to scan the apartment. There were cactus plants of various kinds in every corner. And there were cats, many cats dispersed among the sofas and armchairs. The whole house smelled like cat piss. But, his aunt was already back, was already asking about old relatives, as silent as he was, who didn't even call on the telephone. She came with the enormous family photo album and took a seat on the sofa, next to Danilo.

"Do you want some crème de vie?"

"No, auntie, I don't drink alcohol."

"Just like your mother, may she rest in peace. Nevertheless, she was luckier than me; she got a husband. Just look, look at the photo of your mother when she was fifteen years old. Wasn't she pretty? Now look at me, always closing my mouth so no one would see my cavity-ridden teeth. And this one is grandma Salvadora, and that one is grandpa Papito, and here's your aunt Patria, who married the mailman, and here …"

At that moment, Danilo brought his hand to his stomach and made a grimace.

"What's wrong? Are you ill?"

"Diarrhea, auntie. For the last week, I've had diarrhea."

"Then go to the bathroom, child. Don't lose any time."

She took him by the hand and quickly led him to the toilet, warning him to use the least amount of paper possible and to flush when he was done. Danilo nodded in agreement to everything with an expression of extreme pain. When he was alone in the bathroom, he went directly to the sink and started frantically tapping the tiles. One of them sounded hollow and was nearly loose. It was the tile. The treasure tile. Danilo took a nail clipper out and began to carefully scrape the corners of that tile.

"Damn!" He thought. "This is going to be easier than I expected." He stuck an edge of the nail clipper through a gap and soon the tile was in his hands, clearing the way to the treasure. Danilo plowed his hand in and started to feel around in the hole. From outside, he heard his aunt's voice again, who asked him solicitously,

"All better, son?"

"Almost, auntie."

"I have toilet paper for you here, it must've run out. Can I come in?"

"Not now, auntie. I'm on the toilet."

"That's nonsense. Have you already forgotten that I bathed you until you were 15 years old? I'm coming in. You're like a son to me."

Danilo didn't have time to stand up. His aunt came in at the moment he was taking his hand out of the hiding place with a thick pile of 100 note bills.

"Thief!" His aunt yelled, bringing her hands to her head. "You're nothing more than a vulgar and repulsive thief. Leave that money where it was!"

"Aunt, auntie … forgive me. I need three thousand pesos. It's a matter of life or death."

"Leave! Leave this house or I will call the police!"

"Three thousand, beloved auntie. I'll pay you back in a month."

"Earn it by working for it, you rat. Break your back."

Danilo walked over to her and took her by the shoulders.

"Auntie, you have to understand …"

"I don't understand anything. Police! Police! There's a thief in this house!"

Danilo shook her forcefully by the shoulders, but he couldn't help the fragile woman from escaping from his hands and falling to the floor, knocking her head on the edge of the bathtub with a resounding thump. Immediately, blood ran down her head and her dentures fell out of her mouth.

"Aunt! Auntie!"

Danilo kneeled down before her and tried to revive her by tap-ping her face. He spent a few minutes doing so, until he under-stood that his aunt would never recover from that fall. He took her pulse and knew she was dead. He tried to close her eyes, but these were looking lifelessly at some undefined point on the wall. There was no time to lose. Danilo forgot about the old woman and filled his pockets with bills and jewelry. He had to leave quickly. He was no longer Danilo the teacher, or even Danilo the thief. He was Danilo the murderer, and that, under Cornelio Ro-jas's government, carried the price of the firing squad.

In two steps, he was at the door of the house. He opened it, very carefully, and when he saw there was no one on the stairs, he started to run down the steps toward the street.

Ferryman, ferryman ... you're to blame. Although perhaps the real culprit was Cornelio Rojas whom he ran into on the street, looking at him with grave eyes from a street mural.

It was already too late to see the ferryman. So he would wait until morning, taking refuge in some dark place where the po-lice wouldn't find him. He walked. He walked like a madman through the elegant neighborhood of Los Molinos, looking for the right place to spend the night. The noise of a police siren made him enter the doorway of a large, seemingly uninhabited colonial house. Then it started to rain. A cold, abundant rain, that made him back up against the wall of the house and lean against a slimy door where, inexplicably, there were no Cornelio Rojas posters. Since he was still getting wet, he got closer to the door and noticed that it opened slowly. The siren of another patrol car made him open the door wider and enter on the tips of his toes into a large, high-ceilinged house where in years past some bourgeois family, one of the hundreds who had left the country after Cornelio's arrival, had lived. He lit a match. The house smelled like dried shit, but in the middle of the living room was a velvet sofa that, although moth-eaten, was still a good place to rest. He laid down on it. He was so tired that he immediately fell asleep. He dreamt about the ferryman. He dreamt that he was at last escaping the country and sailing through a calm sea to an island of peaceful black people. He didn't know how long he was there, sleeping. But when he woke up, the sun was already coming through the window and a disheveled woman was standing in front of him, watching him with curiosity.

"Forgive my trespassing," Danilo said. "I didn't know there was anyone in this house. I'll leave."

"You'll do no such thing," the woman said. "You have to go up to the second floor to see Mr. Coro."

"Is that an order?"

"Absolutely," the woman said, brandishing an old, rusty machete. "It's easy to come in here, but leaving is a big problem. Come with me."

Danilo rubbed his eyes with his fists and stood up, smoothing out his shirt.

"I'll say again that I'm sorry. I didn't know that this house ..."

"This house has an owner," the disheveled woman said. "Follow me so you can meet him."

Danilo followed the woman up a spiral staircase covered in dust and rat droppings, and both stopped before a gray door. The disheveled woman gave three light taps, and from inside the room, came an energetic voice that said, "Come in, Cossack."

Danilo and the woman went in. It was also a bare room,

except in the middle was an ordinary desk behind which sat a puny man, wearing suspenders despite being shirtless, and looking aimlessly at the new arrivals from behind round, black glasses.

"Is this our new guest?" The little man asked the disheveled woman.

"It is."

"You slept for twelve hours, my friend. I've been waiting for you since six in the morning. I'm Mr. Coro, and I'm blind because a bandit took out my eyes. But I prefer to tell that story another time."

Coro turned his head toward the disheveled woman and ordered, "You can leave, Cossack, leave me alone with this gentleman ..."

"Danilo Castellanos, at your service. I'd like to take this occasion to ask your forgiveness for having dared enter your house. I was truly exhausted."

"Besides, the police are looking for you," Coro said.

"That's not true," Danilo denied. "I've never had problems with the police."

"Do you believe in chiromancy, Mr. Castellanos?"

"I've never thought about it."

"Let's see, come closer, give me your hands. Through your hands, I will know everything you were, are, and will be."

Danilo Castellanos gave his hands over to the little man, and he felt him begin to study them with his fingers.

"An intellectual," Coro started to say. "You have no children, no wife, no house. And I maintain that you are being pursued by the police. Now I'd like to know: for political reasons?"

"I don't know what you're talking about." Danilo was obstinate. "I've never had any problems with the law."

It was then that the little man's squalid hands grabbed his wrists and began to squeeze with such pressure that Danilo fell to the ground whimpering like a child.

"Who are you, brute?" Cora said with a suddenly sinister voice.

"I am Danilo Castellanos, history teacher at Simón Bolivar high school, I am running from the police because I fear I killed my aunt."

"A vulgar criminal!" Coro exclaimed, releasing him at once, his face full of contempt. "That's not what I need in my bunker. I want political men. Do you understand? Principled people who are always ready to give their lives for their homeland. But you are a vulgar old-lady murderer."

"It's not like that," Danilo clarified. "I didn't kill her with my hands. I accidentally pushed her and she hit her head against the bathtub. In reality, I'm a thief."

"Thieves won't overthrow Cornelio Rojas. You're not useful to me, either."

"In all truth, I've never stolen. I only did so to get three thousand pesos and to hire a boat to leave the country. That's a political act."

"Leave the country? That's something rats do. This is a crucial time when you, more than ever, must stay in the country and fight the dictatorship. Everyone wants to leave the country! No one is capable of mustering up the courage to blow the tyrant's brains out like Brutus and Zeno of Elea did in their time. Those were men. Real men. Would you fire against Cornelio Rojas if you had him in front of you?"

Danilo hesitated before responding.

"I've never killed anyone. But the tyrant, I think I would."

"You'll have time enough to prove it," Coro said with a prophetic air. And then he called, "Madame!"

A very beautiful woman, dressed in a see-through negligee, appeared from behind a closet door.

"What do you think of this, Madame?" Coro inquired.

The Madame studied Danilo's appearance for a while. Then she asked, "Is your penis short or long?"

Flushed, Danilo responded, "Average. I'm an average guy."

"We don't admit anyone here who has less than seven inches."

"That's what I have."

"Do you have money?"

"No."

"You're lying."

Then the woman called out, "Whitey!" And through a side door, came an ugly, heavyset man with a garrote in his hands.

"Check him, Whitey."

It was like being on a butcher counter. The big man took Danilo as if he were a ragdoll, and turned him over, felt him all over, took off his clothes, and proceeded to examine them with extreme meticulousness. In the back pocket of his pants, he found the roll of bills, a gold locket, a pocket watch, also gold, and some diamond earrings. He put everything in front of Coro and, after bowing, took his spot in a corner of the room.

"Was there money, Madame?" Coro asked.

"A fortune!" The woman exclaimed, feeling the booty with lecherous hands. "More than nine thousand pesos in bills and about five thousand in jewels."

"A gift from God," Coro opined. "That means our bunker will

be able to survive for many more months. Regarding Mr. Danilo, let him stay. He doesn't have the nerve of an assassin, but perhaps he'll be infected by the spirit of combat that exists in this house. Let the others come!"

The Madame left the room and quickly returned with a small troop of two men and two women. There was the elusive Melanio Webster, whom Coro introduced as the future minister of propaganda after the fall of Cornelio Rojas. At Coro's insistence, that unimportant-looking little man demonstrated what he did daily in dark movie theaters, public bathrooms, deserted alleyways, and vacant plazas where there was no one watching. His art consisted of wetting a rubber stamp in a small pillow soaked in red ink, and sticking it on any surface until the slogan "Death to Cornelio Rojas" was left imprinted. He had never been caught, but if that should ever happen, he had a cyanide pill as a precautionary measure in his pocket to avoid humiliating blows and brutal interrogations. Then Coro introduced Manzano the poet, a black man dressed in an old frock coat, which despite its being ripped and wrinkled he wore with great dignity. He would become head of the country's union of writers and artists, after the fall of Cornelio Rojas. According to Coro, that black man was as good as Rilke and had written more than two hundred battle hymns, cursing Cornelio Rojas and extolling Coro. He also made us a succinct demonstration of his virtues, singing admirably in a tenor's voice:

"Through lands of gold, I've walked without sorrow
and everywhere I found people that be
in their entirety, completely free,
paying homage to Hermenegildo Coro."

The third person Coro introduced was Nefertiti, a teenager with a sensual face, dressed in a shiny cloak that covered her from the neck to her feet. She was an exotic dancer in the capital's clandestine bars and was famous for moving her hips and gyrating her body with more dexterity than Josephine Baker. Many men had offered her their fortunes to spend a night with her, but that young girl rejected money—for handing herself over, her only condition was that the man must have the courage to join the conspiracy to kill Cornelio Rojas. As soon as they heard that, the most braggadocio of men would quickly distance themselves from her and would never proposition her again. She was, therefore, a virgin. Although when it came to masculine genitals, she had been an expert with her mouth since the age of eleven. She also gave a brief demonstration of her art, removing her cloak slowly and dancing a few steps completely nude before Danilo's bulging eyes.

"That's enough!" Coro grumbled from his desk, bitter because his blindness prevented him from seeing the magnificent show.

"Get dressed and go to the foyer to await orders."

Nefertiti put on her cloak quickly and left the room, but not before going over to Coro and giving his thigh an electrifying caress.

"My big, big boy," she said in his ear. "Your every word is sacred to me."

And she left. Coro remained in his chair, his shoulders slumped, looking toward the ceiling with an expression of intense sadness.

"Cossack …," he then said: "Go see what Cornelio Rojas is doing right now."

The disheveled woman took a compact from between her breasts, and opened it with the utmost care. Then, she took out a cotton ball that she wet with saliva, and rubbed it three times over the oval-shaped mirror. After a few seconds of complete concentration, the woman informed him:

"Now, I see Cornelio Rojas on a luxurious yacht, surrounded by young, semi-clad women, who are fighting among themselves to put lotion on his thighs and shoulders and to comb his beard."

"The vile man!" Coro said, in a rage. "That yacht should've been mine. Those women belong to me. He stole everything from me! This revolution was mine, mine. Do you understand, Mr. Danilo Castellanos? I was the strongman who was going to come to power thirty-two years ago. Cornelio Rojas was no more than a lady-in-waiting to whom I transmitted my wisdom and political projects from a little plaza set beside the University's law school. Back then, I wasn't blind. It was enough for me to stare firmly at men for them to obey me without hesitation. I already had a clandestine army of fifty young men willing to die for me. I had already developed the plan to attack the presidential palace and execute President Estrada. The date for the action had been set. And one day, Mr. Castellanos, when I was alone in that same little plaza, pondering the final touches of our attack, a masked son of a bitch—surely Cornelio Rojas himself—came out from behind some trees and, with two fingers as hard as nails, took my eyes out in one blow. I was left blind. Do you understand, Castellanos? Blind!" As he said this, Coro removed his dark glasses and showed Danilo his horrible, empty sockets that still oozed blood.

"Afterwards …," he continued, in a serious voice, "history continued on its course. From the hospital where I was, I found out a coup d'état had been carried out. President Estrada had been killed. People were out in the streets cheering for the young, courageous men who had overthrown the Yankee puppet. And the leader of the revolution was none other than that lady-in-waiting Cornelio Rojas. Since then, thirty years have passed. Thirty years of him giving my speeches, enacting my laws, applying my foreign policy, doing at last all that I had taught him on those calm afternoons in the little University Plaza. Today Cornelio Rojas is a God while the train of history has rolled over me, crushing my bones."

"There's still time, my boy," the Madame said enthusiastically.

"Perhaps," Coro admitted. "I only need a firm grip, a heart of steel, and a lofty spirit capable of sending two explosive bullets into that revolting head."

"That's difficult," Danilo dared to say. "Cornelio Rojas is surrounded day and night by a strong security apparatus."

"Nonsense!" Coro said. "Every day a president gets killed. Besides, I have Cossack, who is capable of seeing even further than eagles. Let's see, Cossack, what is that charlatan doing now?"

Cossack rubbed the mirror in her compact again and a few seconds later revealed, "He's deep-sea fishing. He caught an enormous swordfish and is bringing him to the surface right now."

"Deep-sea fishing, delectable women, beach houses, power and glory … all mine! Mine!"

Coro banged the desk violently and started to whine like a child who has been denied a piece of candy.

"All of you out!" He suddenly yelled. "Leave me alone. I want to again analyze the plan we made. Out!"

The small troop left the room in a single file and all of them dispersed to different corners awaiting new orders. Danilo and the Madame sat down on the worn-out sofa and looked at each other in silence for a long while.

"Do you like me?" the Madame suddenly asked, reaching one hand toward Danilo's chest and caressing his nipples.

"Very much," the young man responded, beginning to shake thanks to the wanderings of that electrifying hand.

"Do you want to make love to me?" the woman continued, lowering her hand to Danilo's abdomen.

"Here? In front of everyone?"

"Don't be silly. This house has seven rooms and 24 closets. Count to 100 with your eyes closed, and when you're finished, come find me, I'll be waiting for you someplace to become yours. Close your eyes and start counting."

Danilo closed his eyes and counted to one hundred without skipping. When he finished, the Madame had disappeared. The only trace of her was the strong smell of violets.

Following that scent, Danilo went up the spiral staircase and opened the first door he found. There were only books there, moth-eaten books with the spines detached. He opened the closet and found more books. Nonetheless, the trace of the Madame's perfume indicated she had been through there. He left the room and went to the following one, where the scent of violets also floated. But the Madame wasn't there either. In her place was a crocodile tied to the wall who attacked Danilo when he approached it to get a better look. The third room was a small Napoleonic Museum. There was the death mask Napoleon's head doctor had made of him, a bicorn with the colors of France, some letters from Napoleon to Josephine signed in

Egypt, sabers, guns, and an enormous portrait of Napoleon on horseback made by some period artist. The Madame had also been there and her scent lead the young man to the contiguous room where there were dozens of hens pecking at bread crumbs and laying their eggs in nests made of old clothes. The other two rooms were empty. Danilo opened their closets and found several intact skeletons and mountains of skulls and loose bones. The Madame had also been through there. There was just one last room to search, and Danilo had the feeling that the game was coming to an end. The woman had to be there. He opened the seventh room, and found himself in Coro's room where, as a matter fact, the woman was seated on the blind man's knees, caressing his incipient bald spot and kissing his forehead with maternal devotion.

"Who entered?" Coro asked the woman.

"It's Mr. Castellanos, who wants to fornicate with me."

"Ah!" Coro exclaimed with a ferocious smile. "That has to be earned my dear friend. In this bunker only the courageous have the right to love. But that speaks well of you. Sex and courage go together, I guarantee it. Perhaps you're not what you seem. Let's see."

Then Coro called out,

"Whitey!" And from the side closet came the big, hairy man, who looked at Danilo with eyes full of hate and planted himself before him, ready for a fight.

"Break his bones, Whitey. Let's see how far courage gets this old-lady murderer."

Coro clapped his hands and Whitey leapt on Danilo, knocking him over immediately, and began beating him on the floor.

"I surrender, I surrender," Danilo blubbered with his nose broken by a punch. "I can't take on this man. He's stronger than I am."

When he heard this, Coro broke into sinister laughter and again ordered his thug,

"Rape him, Whitey. Take over that faggot's ass; he doesn't deserve to belong in the world of men."

Danilo backed up against the wall, asking everyone for mercy. He was a coward, he confessed, but he had never given his ass to anyone. Whitey didn't pay attention to his pleas. He threw Danilo to the ground again and with precise motions removed all of Danilo's clothes. But something must've happened within Danilo's soul when his virginity was endangered. Something annihilated his cowardice and infuriated him. He delivered a blow to Whitey's head, and Whitey stepped back, surprised. Then Danilo delivered a kick to the big man's testicles that made him double over in pain. Without wasting any time, Danilo grabbed an iron chair and brought it down on Whitey's head, making him fall to the floor unconscious.

Coro, duly informed by the Madame of each step of the fight, applauded Danilo's victory for a few seconds.

"Do you see, Mr. Castellanos? You're capable of defending your ass like a tiger, and yet you're not capable of reacting the same way to the daily rape to which Cornelio Rojas subjects you. Don't you live like a dog? Isn't it enough that the tyrant violates your most basic rights daily? You can't speak freely. You can't read whatever you like, you can't travel around the world, you have to go to the agricultural fields without complaint, as the tyrant demands. You eat only potatoes and eggs, the only things that are abundant in this country. You have already been raped, my dear friend. Your only redemption is to participate in this conspiracy to execute Cornelio Rojas. Take this!"

And Coro removed a Colt 45 pistol from a drawer and handed it to Danilo.

"Play with it," Coro continued. "Practice your aim killing rats in the basement. Imagine that each smoked rat is Cornelio Rojas himself. Take it, caress it, remember that God made each man different, but that that Colt makes them equal forever."

"What do you want from me?" Danilo asked holding the beautiful pistol in his hands.

"I'll tell you," Coro said. "In two days, Cornelio Rojas and the Arab tyrant Moammar Qaddafi will be part of a convoy four blocks from here. They'll go slowly because both characters like the fanfare, and being cheered on by the crowd. You will be posted on the corner of First and Fourth, blending in with the large crowd that will go to pay homage to both tyrants. You need to stay in the heat of the moment, keep your pulse firm, and your eyes on the prize. When the convoy is just a few steps away from you, you will take the weapon from your waist and shoot the nine explosive bullets loaded in the pistol. You will die without a doubt. But it will be a much more dignified death, a thousand times more elegant, than the firing squad death awaiting you for killing an old woman."

Danilo remained pensive for a few seconds. "Ferryman, ferryman, you're to blame."

"I can't," the young man reacted brusquely, putting the pistol back in Coro's hands.

"Come on, don't be a coward. I guarantee that you will be remembered forever by the people as the savior of our national dignity. Statues all over the place, your name in the history books, ballads that troubadours will sing in every town. A magnificent end! I envy you."

"I'm not interested in any of that. I want to live. Do you understand? I want to live!"

"Fine, there you have the door to the street. You can do what you want. Go out, I assure you that in less than an hour you will be behind bars, surrounded by miscreants of the worst kind and, what's worse, awaiting your death in some dark prison courtyard."

Danilo hung his head in his hands and moaned softly.

"Don't cry, Castellanos. If I still had my eyes, I wouldn't hesitate to act."

"I just can't. Send someone else."

"Someone else would be impossible. Melanio Webster is nervous and would shoot before it was time. Manzano the poet is very manly, but he's half-mad and would stand out with his wrinkled frock coat and enormous Afro. Whitey is a good soldier, but he's clumsy and only acts when he hears my voice. I wouldn't be there. I could only utter some curse at the tyrant that would get lost amid all the people's voices. That leaves just you, my friend. And you only have two days to decide.

When he said this, Coro handed the pistol back to Danilo and ordered the Madame to take him to the basement to practice his aim.

The woman took Danilo by the arm and led him out of the room, giving him an encouraging pat on the back.

"There's more for you, darling," the Madame whispered in the young man's ear. "If you accept the role of assassin, you'll have the right to deflower Nefertiti, the most sought-after little whore in every bar of the port."

They went down rickety stairs to the damp, dark basement that smelled of rats. The Madame lit an oil lamp and immediately hundreds of rats started to shriek and run from side to side, fleeing from the light.

"Let's go," the Madame said. "Fire on them. Try to kill as many as you can. Imagine that each rat is Cornelio Rojas and take out all of your hate on them. Shoot!"

Danilo aimed at a rat that was gnawing on an old shoe. He shot.

"Good shot," the Madame said. "You pulverized him. Shoot, shoot, I brought enough ammunition in my pocket."

Danilo began to shoot left and right. Sometimes he missed, but most of the time he made a direct shot on the vermin who were scattering in all directions through the holes in the walls. When the ammunition ran out, the Madame counted the dead rats. There were eleven.

"Good aim," the woman said.

"When I was a boy, I shot birds with a shotgun." Danilo explained.

"Magnificent!" the Madame exclaimed. "Coro should know that."

"Does Coro need to know everything?"

"Everything. Coro is my official husband. We were married before a notary. My soul belongs to him. And only my soul, because I can do whatever I want with my body." And with that, the Madame undid the straps of her dress, and was completely naked before Danilo's eyes.

She had the monumental figure of a Greek goddess. Little by little, she undressed Danilo and they ended up rolling around on the damp floor, merged together in an embrace of legs and arms as they bit each other like fiends.

"That's enough," the Madame said when they achieved their fourth orgasm. "You're a real man. Another reason to trust you with the mission we've given you."

They got dressed and left the basement, holding on to each other's waists. Danilo Castellanos placed the pistol at his hip. He was starting to receive the privileges that only the most manly of men were given. He was definitely now a member of the bunker. Perhaps the most important one from now on.

That night Danilo Castellanos didn't sleep. He laid on the tattered sofa going over all the day's events. Coro was right. Cornelio Rojas had raped the country's boldest men, stealing their freedom. A suicidal act was necessary, but somebody who would grow some balls and execute the tyrant despite the risk. Danilo pondered the pistol in his hand for a long time, and remembered a story by Borges. It was the story of a dying man who was complaining before God of the stupid end he would endure in a low-end hospital bed. God then saved him and sent him to the South, where the land was hot and men fought each other for the pleasure of seeing blood. There a cattle farmer killed him with one shot in a duel and the young man had the dignified death he had requested of the divine. Danilo Castellanos was now in a similar situation. Did life really matter to him in that enormous jail that was his country? How long would he keep dealing with his own fear and withstanding the dictatorship of that cruel man? Yes, he had to kill him. He had to accept the idea that the story of the South was a good one and to face death once and for all instead of dying every day.

When the sun rose he went up the stairs directly to Coro's room. There was everyone; waiting for him, for his final word, for his decision.

He went over to Coro and said in a resolute voice:

"You have convinced me. I will kill Cornelio Rojas."

The group immediately burst into applause; it lasted several minutes. Coro stood up from his chair and went over to Danilo to kiss him on the cheek. The women threw themselves at him and kissed him long on the mouth. Yes, his fate was decided. Danilo Castellanos had chosen the Borgesian South over the slave's life he had been leading for thirty years.

When the applause ended, Danilo asked Cossack to give him a new report on what Cornelio Rojas was doing just then.

After the ritual with the compact and the cotton ball, Cossack revealed:

"Cornelio Rojas is in a pool right now with his extraordinary guest, Moammar Qaddafi. Young women dressed as ancient Romans are pouring bottles and bottles of champagne over both men's heads."

"Enjoy it, enjoy it," Coro said meanly. "Enjoy it, Cornelio, since you don't have much time left."

The Madame turned on her wireless radio, and the announcer could be heard telling the people to gather the next day along First Street to welcome our friend Qaddafi and to wildly applaud Cornelio Rojas.

"Grab your flag and your poster, and show up at eleven a.m. sharp on First Street. It's a question of honor. Don't miss it."

"We'll be there," Coro commented. And, turning to Danilo with an obsequious smile, he wanted to know:

"What would you like now, my prince? All of the women in this house belong to you for 24 hours. Or perhaps you'd like to drink to delirium. Or perhaps you'd like to practice the action you'll be involved in, live."

"What do you mean?" Danilo asked.

"A pantomime," Cora said. "A dramatic representation of what you will do tomorrow on the corner of First Street." And, turning toward the bunker's members Coro enthusiastically ordered:

"Come on, all of you, make a line across this room, simulating the line of people who will applaud for Cornelio Rojas. You, Whitey, go to the crocodile room and put on the uniform with gold decorations. You'll come into this room again when I call for you. Go!"

Whitey disappeared through the door and the rest of the conspirators made a line across the room and started to yell "Cornelio, Cornelio, we love Cornelio!" Danilo stood at the end of the line with the pistol at his hip.

"Are you ready, my prince?" Coro asked.

"Ready," Danilo answered firmly.

Then two knocks came at the door, and Coro, who was the first one in line, said in a resounding voice:

"Enter, Cornelio Rojas!"

Whitey came in dressed in a uniform very similar to the one Cornelio Rojas always wore. All of them started to applaud and to yell "Cornelio, Cornelio, we love Cornelio!"

Whitey moved forward with very short steps and paraded in front of Coro, waving and smiling. Then he passed in front of Cossack and the Madame, who threw kisses at him with the tips of their fingers. He passed in front of Manzano the poet, before Melanio, before Nefertiti, but when he passed before Danilo, the latter took the pistol from his hip and planted himself in front of Whitey with a face full of hate.

He was supposed to imitate the shots with his mouth, but Danilo's rage was such and he was playing the role with so much passion, that he pulled the pistol's trigger and the bullet wounded Whitey in the foot.

"Fool! Fool!" Coro howled when he heard the shot. "You shot for real. You wounded Whitey. And what's worse, the noise could have been heard by anyone. You, Cossack, go to the window and see if there are any busybodies milling about. You, Madame, tend to Whitey's wound however you can. And you, Castellanos, give me that pistol. I'll give it back to you a few minutes before we go to action. You're a fool."

Cossack went out to the street and came back with disturbing news. There was a patrol car on the corner, and the police kept looking at the house.

"Fine," Coro said, bitterly. "They've discovered us. It's this bunker's last hour. We made an oath one day and will see it through now. We'll die before we become Cornelio Rojas's prisoners."

Then, Coro took a bottle of white pills out of the drawer and started handing them out one by one to the bunkers members.

"Cyanide," Coro said when he gave Danilo his pill. "Don't swallow it. Don't chew it. Just let it dissolve in your mouth. In five seconds we will all die."

Danilo took the pill with an air of seriousness, and accepted that there was no possible alternative. Through his mistake, the assassination would not be carried out. That was what bothered him so intensely. Much more than dying of poison.

Coro took his pill with two fingers and gave the last order of his life,

"Ready? Set? Go!"

And they all put the pills in their mouths and waited, livid and silent, for death's arrival. Ten, fifteen, thirty seconds passed, until Coro let out another one of his terrible guffaws and exclaimed, "Gentlemen, what a bunker I have here! What loyalty to your principles! What courage under fire! Don't worry, comrades, it was just aspirin. But keep in mind that someday if the police dare to enter this room, they will only find the corpses of nine courageous people."

Cossack dispelled any remaining tension when she went back out to the street and returned with the news that the patrol car had left.

"God is with us," Coro said. "You, Madame, put on some music. You, Nefertiti, dance for everyone. May these last hours be filled with enjoyment and happiness. Rum! Bring the rum!"

Again, it was Cossack who left the room and came back dragging a box of liquor.

"Hand it out, hand it out," Coro said. "Let everyone drink, let everyone laugh, let everyone fornicate."

An hour later, Coro's room looked like a Roman hall in the time of Caligula. Salsa music was playing, the people were emptying bottles in three swigs and opening more. Manzano the poet was rolling around in the corner with Cossack. The Madame was riding Coro's flanks completely naked. Melanio Webster, Whitey, and Danilo watched Nefertiti's striptease in fascination, as she moved her hips with more panache than the fabulous Tongolele. Thus, dancing, the adolescent girl went over to Danilo and started to remove his shirt.

"Macho, macho man. Do you swear that tomorrow you will kill that infamous Cornelio Rojas?"

"The die is cast." Danilo responded with conviction.

"Then take me, my King. Make me remember you forever."

They both fell down on a bed of old newspapers and Danilo, his penis hard as an elephant hunter's sword, broke Nefertiti's resistant membrane with one resolute push and merged with her in a bloody, but delicious, embrace, that reached an other-worldly delirium as the girl contorted her hips on the floor like a lusty salamander.

Thus they spent the last night, until six in the morning when Coro woke them all up with the national anthem blasting on the radio, and the exciting news that there were only five hours left for the country's history to take a 180 degree turn.

"Danilo, macho man, do you still have your courage?"

"Give me the pistol," Danilo answered firmly.

Coro gave him the weapon and Danilo felt it once more at his hip, again transmitting a pleasant sensation of power. He studied the chamber and counted nine bullets. If just one of them entered Cornelio's head, that would be enough. And if Qaddafi misbehaved, another bullet would be for him.

The Madame turned up the volume on the battery-operated radio and the announcer's voice came on again, informing them that there were more than a million people lined up along the streets through which the convoy would pass.

"Grab your flag and your poster and show up at this act of in-ternational solidarity. Let's show the world that our revolution is invincible and that our people march with conviction alongside our Maximum Leader."

"They must've left the capital building already," Coro reasoned. "Traveling fifteen miles an hour, it's possible they'll pass by the fatal corner at noon. What time is it?"

"Nine," the Madame said.

"Well," Coro summarized. "We'll leave here at eleven. You, Danilo, the most macho of all machos, do you have a final wish?"

"Yes. I want to bathe, put on clean clothes, and, if possible, shave and put on a lot of cologne."

"Madame," Coro said. "Make sure you give him a good bath. Look in the closet for some clean shirts and look for a bottle of Brut cologne among my belongings."

The Madame took Danilo by the arm and led him gently to one of the bathrooms, the cleanest one, since the others were clogged and the toilets overflowed with filth.

"You manly man," the Madame said once they were both in the bathroom. "What an honor to bathe you, you who will make me free in two hours. Can I kiss your wee-wee?"

"Do it," Danilo said. He was terse, had a vague look on his face and the nervous tic in his eyes had come back along with the ulcer pain.

"I'm going to die, dammit," Danilo whispered.

"You will never die completely," the Madame said as she began to soap him up with a sponge.

"Ferryman, ferryman … all of it is the fault of that damned ferryman."

"Has your resolve weakened again? Are you feeling afraid again?"

"No," Danilo said. And he repeated, firmly, "The die is cast."

Once he was dry, dressed and perfumed, he took the beautiful pistol in his hands and thought about the most unfortunate events of his life. He couldn't find one day of happiness among his memories. Cornelio Rojas had robbed him of thirty years of freedom. Thirty years in which he had imposed the law of his balls on the people and had crushed all rebellion.

No, Danilo wasn't feeling cowardly. Rather, he was impatient to have the tyrant before him to empty the contents of the pistol into his head.

"You look so handsome!" the Madame said when she saw him dressed up and coiffed. "You look worthy of a photo."

"I don't want any photos. What I want is for all of this to happen quickly, and that my death be immediate. But only after seeing him fall over with a bullet in his head."

"That's how real men talk," the Madame said. "Come on, let's go back to Coro's room."

They went out. In Coro's room, everyone was listening to the radio. The announcer informed them that Cornelio Rojas's convoy had just entered First Avenue.

"We've got him within our reach now," Coro said. "Cossack, hand out the flags and the posters of the tyrant. We all have to keep a distance of two meters. Go on out. Quickly!"

One by one, they started exiting the old house, carrying flags and posters of Cornelio Rojas. Down Fourth Street came waves of people yelling happily,

"Cornelio, Cornelio, we love Cornelio!"

The conspirators joined the masses and started to approach the corner of attack. When they arrived at the site, they all placed themselves in the front line, near Danilo, who more than ever, felt the cold pistol under his shirt. Suddenly, the clamor rose. On the main street, Cornelio Rojas's convertible limousine appeared in the distance, surrounded by dozens of plainclothes policeman who were looking all around them like mad dogs.

"Are you feeling confident, big guy?" Coro said into Danilo's ear.

"My fate is sealed," was the young man's response.

A few steps away, Cossack made the sign of the cross discreetly so the crowd wouldn't see her. The Madame gave Danilo a last kiss on the ear. Melanio Webster, who knew how to draw, was trying to quickly capture Danilo's tense face with charcoal and some paper.

The convoy got closer. The flags waved happily and pictures of Cornelio were raised by hundreds of joyous hands.

And then something happened. Something that was not in the bunker inhabitants plans. A block before arriving at Danilo's corner, Cornelio Rojas and Qaddafi got out of the limousine and started to walk between the two rows of cheering people. They talked to the people, kissed several children, and shook hands with some old men. In the blink of an eye, Danilo Castellanos found himself before Cornelio Rojas in the flesh and the tyrant was looking at him—his eyes radiating confidence and self-assuredness. Breathing with aplomb, knowing he was in absolute control of the situation, Cornelio leaned over to kiss a newborn, caressed the white hair of a teary-eyed old woman, gave a cigar to an old man leaning on a cane who seemed a hundred years old, and suddenly, he extended a soft, warm hand to Danilo.

"And you? What do you do for the homeland, my fellow countryman?"

"I'm a high school history teacher."

"Keep fighting then, my fellow countryman. The revolution needs many men like you."

He withdrew his hand. Danilo slumped over and, for a few seconds, felt he was about to pass out. He was afraid that the pistol could be seen through his shirt. But no, the crucial moment had already passed. The opportunity of a lifetime had been squandered. Cornelio Rojas and Moammar Qaddafi got into the limousine again, and continued at high speed toward the presidential palace. The groups dispersed. Danilo hung his head and started to walk to Coro's big house as if he were a zombie. Then he felt a kick in his shin: it was Cossack. A bump to the head: it was Whitey; spit on his face: it was the Madame. The horrendous insults in his ear came from Nefertiti. The foot stepping on his was Melanio Webster's, and Coro's shadowy guffaw announced terrible punishment and humiliation. He continued walking slowly, without protest, toward the old, colonial style house that was the last bastion of resistance against tyranny. His resolve had weakened. Now they would always call him "the Rat," and he would live with the rats, in the filthy basement, eating on the floor and sleeping over puddles of putrid water.

But all was not lost. The following month would bring the arrival of Yasser Arafat, the Palestinian leader. Another parade like this one would promenade down one of the city's main streets. Perhaps then. Perhaps then!